LAURA LUKASAVAGE

See You On The Other Side

First edition

ISBN: 978-1-7366905-4-3

Cover art by River Author Service's
Editing by Josie

This book was professionally typeset on Reedsy.
Find out more at reedsy.com

For my Aunt Mary, godmother, friend and confidant. Like so many others, you were taken too soon. I will miss you every day. Thank you for always building me up and for being someone I could confide in. Say hello to my parents for me and everyone else. Rest in peace with all the other angels. Until we meet again.

Contents

Acknowledgments

Thank you to the beautiful Josie for working so hard to help me make my work better than it was before, blessed to have met you.

And a special thank you to all of you, MY READERS, who make my dream a reality. I can only grow in my writing and dreams and I hope you will stick around for the ride! Much more to come!!!!

Going Home

Jane

As I approach my new suburban home, I feel the darkness moving in around me. Uneasy and afraid of what's coming next. An uncontrollable force takes hold of me, causing my body to feel like it's chained by thousands of rocks holding me tightly in my place.

Who would have thought that only an hour ago, I had everything I ever wanted and prayed for? Now, it's all being ripped from my fingers.

I glance down at my right hand lingering on the scuffed-up old doorknob. Sam and I bought this house only a few months ago, anticipating that everything would fall into place once we married. He told me he wanted to give me the life he felt I always deserved. Sam understood what I wanted from life, even if it was something I never spoke aloud. He knew I wanted: to get married, so he made it happen. He knew I always wanted a suburban home, so he found us one. I still remember his words that day after showing it to me for the first time.

"This is only the beginning. I want you to have the life and family you always imagined, and I will do my best to make it happen for us. You deserve all of this, and so much more."

Sam always found ways to remind me how meeting me had redeemed him. It took him years to admit how low he had sunk, no longer recognizing the person he had become. We had known each other for over a year before he noticed the positive change before he felt his old self breaking through. He noticed the shift began when he met me. He told me that my simply being there for him to talk to was all he needed. Someone who cared enough to sit and listen to what was eating away silently at his soul. He said it was my faith and my strength that helped him find his way back, and that it was something he would never forget.

Frozen outside my front door, I glance around, taking in my surroundings while trying to convert them to my memory. The outside of the house had always been my favorite. When Sam showed me our new home for the first time, I realized how well he really knew me and how much he paid attention to the little things I would say. I had mentioned to him once how I always wanted a home where the outside was made of a beautiful assortment of bricks, and that's what our home has. Deep crimson and fawn in color. The bricks give the house the character that I have come to love so much.

A smile creeps onto my face as I look above my head and see the tan-colored awning. Sam thought through everything when he bought this house. The canopy comes out overhead far enough to cover your whole body from the sun and weather.

I peek over my right shoulder to take notice of Sam's black Toyota in the driveway and I know he's still home, which doesn't surprise me. Sam owns the biggest restaurant in town and being the owner, he can choose when he wants to go in. I always liked the idea of marrying a man who could cook, so I wasn't always the one doing it. I never thought I would marry someone who owned their own restaurant and was a better cook than me.

Lost in my thoughts, I close my eyes and take in a breath, waiting for my lungs to expand like a balloon filling with water. When they do not, I open my eyes and release the air in one quick motion. I turn the knob, pushing the door open quietly as I take my first step through the threshold. The familiar smell of fresh roses and garlic chicken overwhelms my senses. These smells have become ones that I associate with Sam and my home. I close my eyes quickly to protect them from the blinding white light entering the room from between the two-inch gaps in the blinds. I wait a few seconds before trying to open them again. When I finally do, I hear the door make a light-clicking noise behind me. It would have closed sooner if it were not for the bronze-colored rug sitting on the floor in front of the door. I personally cannot stand it being there, but Sam won the argument saying it was smart to have in case our shoes were slippery from the weather one day coming home. It made more sense to have it than to end up on my butt one day.

I scan the room and my eyes come to rest on the fresh crimson roses that sit across the way in their new home inside my favorite sapphire vase. Sam put them on my working desk to make sure I would notice them. I smile at the thought of him picking them up this morning. I look all around the house trying to soak it all into my memory. The spot on the ceiling right above our tan coach draws my attention. The crack is so noticeable that it makes me smile. Sam has told me on more than one occasion that he would fix it, but it is still there. It never really bothered me much. I honestly like the fact that he would forget to do things. It made me remember that he isn't perfect and he's human just like me. For the longest time, I always thought he was too good to be true, that he couldn't be human because he was always so good at everything he did.

I continue to scan the room until I come across the pictures of me and my family; my two sisters, Mom and Dad sitting on the shelf next to the 65-inch TV. My eyes continue to wander until I see the picture of Sam with his two sisters and parents and then finally, I see our wedding photo. It's hard to believe we were only married eight months ago, in late August. It puts a smile on my face now to think about all the times our families would tell us we were too young to get married. Sam was twenty-five and I was only twenty-two, but we knew it the moment we met three years ago that we were meant to be in each other's lives forever.

He had just come out of a horrible breakup. She was the only girl he ever really loved, and he had been with her for ten years. He would tell me all the time that it was his fault, and he didn't treat her right and how she was the best girl he ever knew. When we met, he was in a dark place, feeling the emptiness of her loss. She had left him only a month before. I was also in my own personal hell of a relationship, and I couldn't see how the man I was with was my downfall. While I helped Sam find his way slowly back to a place of peace, he also showed me how a man should treat a woman and that I was not being treated right. Somewhere in between everything we were dealing with, things shifted between us and I still couldn't tell you for sure when it happened or who changed it first. All that matters is we found each other and for the last few years, I've been happier than I ever have in my life, and I wouldn't change a thing.

"Jane, is that you?"

Sam's voice echoes through the house to my awaiting ears as the curve of my mouth lifts and the lines of my face reach my eyes. Seconds later, I see him standing at the top of the spiral staircase. My hazel eyes connect with his jade ones as they shine in the sunlight. His hair, just long enough for you to run your fingers through, is damp, making it almost raven in color. His lightly chapped lips part as a smile spreads over his face as he descends the staircase. I do not move as he runs down them at full speed. When he reaches me, he wraps his long firm arms around me. Towering over me at 6'3", he bends down to lay his face in my hair as he takes in a deep breath that makes my smile grow.

"You always smell like lavender." He pulls away and looks down at me with a smile still plastered on his face.

His scar-filled hands leave my waist to cup my warm cheeks as he draws me in for a kiss. Even covered in scars from cooking in the restaurant, his skin is still gentle to the touch. His lips are firm against mine and they feel like home. Every minute of every day I could be happy if this were all we had; knowing he loves me and needs me like I need him, needing each other like our lungs need air.

That would have been more than enough for me.

Sam pulls away, ending our embrace, but his hands linger on my cheeks as his expression turns to one of concern, "Not that I don't love seeing you but what are you doing home so early?"

Not ready to tell him yet, I lie, "My shift ended."

I see the questions lingering in his lime eyes, "But you just left for the hospital a few hours ago. You've never had a shift that short before."

My hands begin to tremble as my body convulses and I feel the moisture running down my face off my forehead. A look of pure concern embeds itself into Sam's facial features as he removes his hands from my face to take mine in his.

"Jane, what is it? What's wrong?"

I release a long-repressed sigh as I motion with my head to the couch. "Can we sit down?"

Sam's hands slide up my arms and become firm as he looks me in the eyes. "Please, don't make me ask again."

I look away from him towards the window not sure what to say next. "Please, sit down."

He reluctantly releases my arms and grabs my hand once more to pull me with him towards the couch. He sits and tries to pull me down next to him.

"I think I want to stand."

Sam hesitantly releases my hand. "OK."

I am unsure of how to proceed. I mean, how am I supposed to tell him? There is no easy way, but I don't want to just blurt it out. I cannot. How can I make this news any easier for him? Is there even a way? What if it was me? What if things were reversed? I know there would be nothing he could say to make it easier, nothing I would want to hear, nothing I could hear. I look down at him and his pleading face.

I take in a deep breath as I look him in the eyes and blurt out the words before my nerves stop me once more, "I'm dead."

Sam, startling me, jumps up off the couch as if he were just punched in the gut. I see anger forming in his features as his hands become fists at his sides, knuckles whitening in protest. "Jane, that isn't funny."

"I'm not trying to be funny," I reply sadly.

"You're tired, you need a break. You are thinking things that aren't real."

He reaches for me with his hand.

I shake my head back and forth and ignore his arm outstretched for me. "I wish that's all it was. I wish I could tell you I was only tired."

He reaches my side and takes my hands in his. "Babe, you've been working long hours the last few weeks. That's all it is."

I look up into his anxiety-ridden eyes. "No, Sam. I'm being serious."

He shakes his head like he is trying to clean out the cobwebs. "Jane. This is crazy. Do you realize how crazy you're sounding right now?"

I glance down at our interlocked hands. "Yes."

"Why would you even say something like that to me?"

I gaze into his sad eyes. "Because as much as it hurts it's the truth."

"It can't be." He says in an exhausted tone.

I release a repressed sigh. "But it is."

"How?"

"There was a blood vessel in my brain. It popped this morning when I went to work. There was nothing they could do."

"No. You're here. You're standing right here in front of me." He runs his fingers down my cheek and I close my eyes to his touch, "And I can touch you. It was only a bad dream. One of those vivid ones."

"It wasn't a dream," I whisper in a shaky voice.

"It's not possible. What you're saying isn't possible." He releases my hands and turns his back to me. "Unless what you are trying to tell me is that you died but they brought you back. You were dead, but now you're ok." He peers over his shoulder to look in my direction.

I shake my head back and forth.

He closes the distance between us once again. "But you're here with me, you're fine."

"That's the thing. I came to say goodbye."

Sam looks at me as though I have lost my mind. "What?"

"You can see me and touch me because they gave us this time so that I could," I pause, "so that I could break the news to you, to try to make this easier; kind of like you're having a dream of me and I'm not really here."

"No. No, babe, maybe you bumped your head or something or you thought something happened that didn't." He chuckles nervously, "Or maybe we are both dreaming."

"I wish that were the case." I look down and close my eyes before I say, "Soon they will call you and tell you what happened." I look back up at his pain-filled eyes. "I'm so sorry. I don't want to leave. Not when we just started our forever."

My tears take my breath away and I can't form another word. I feel the warm moisture making its way down my cheeks in a waterfall of tears, and as hard as I try to stop them from coming, it is to no avail. My breathing slows as my lungs beg for air that will never come.

The thought of leaving him behind so soon after our lives together have started is killing me. Knowing that I will never have the chance to grow old with him or have his children. Knowing I will never know the feeling of our baby kicking inside of me or getting to see my child after many long painful hours of childbirth. All the things I wanted and dreamed about were lost to me– gone. I won't get to share those moments with him. I won't be able to help him through his grief, not this time.

I am raging with anger. I can feel the heat rising to the surface of my skin as the anger begins to consume me from the inside out. This isn't fair, it isn't right. I'm only twenty-two years old. I am too young to die.

Sam can see the anger building up inside of me as he pulls me into his arms and holds me in a tight embrace. "You are fine, you're here with me and you're fine."

I grab a fistful of his maroon long-sleeve flannel shirt as I mumble into his chest. "Nothing about this is fine."

"Stop thinking about it." He whispers into the top of my head.

I bury my face deeper into the fabric of his shirt. "How can I? I am dead. I'm dead and I can't change that."

"You are fine. Just breathe. I've got you."

I pull away from him and look up to see his jade eyes shining as I see the moisture starting to take refuge in them. I was going to argue further with him, but I could see that he knew something was not right, but he didn't want to believe it.

I force a smile and lay my head back on his chest and whisper into his shoulder. "I love you."

His arms go tight around my back. "I love you too."

RING. RING. RING. RING.

Every ring feels like an eternity. I know this is it and I'm torn. I don't want to leave; I shouldn't have to leave. I cannot say goodbye and walk away. I can't leave him alone in this. I remember how bad he got when he lost his ex and I can only imagine how losing me, his wife, is going to affect him. We were supposed to have the rest of our lives together.

Sam starts to walk over to the phone then stops to look back at me. I am confused as to why until he looks down at our intertwined hands with a sad smile. I would not let it go; I wouldn't let him go. I force a smile of my own and slowly release his hand.

"Sam."

He stops.

"Please. Don't forget me, and do not forget who you are. Don't lose sight of the man I fell in love with. Don't lose your faith, your drive, and your ambition. Don't lose you...OK?"

The lines on his face go slack, and I can see he is trying to think of something to say back but the phone rings again and with it, all his thoughts evaporate into the air around him. He turns his back to me.

As he reaches for the phone I whisper, "I love you, don't ever forget that."

I know he heard me because he starts to turn around but changes his mind at the last moment as he places the phone against his ear.

"Hello...This is he."

My body feels heavy again like it is being infused with concrete. The weight of it brings me to my knees as I close my arms around my body trying to hold myself together. I glance in Sam's direction. There is so much I will miss about him. Like the way his chocolate-colored hair lays just below his ears in a way that always makes me want to run my fingers through it. The way his emerald eyes shine when I enter the room, the way the right corner of his mouth lifts when he starts to smile.

My body feels like it's fading into nothing as I watch the conversation taking place between Sam and the person on the other end of the phone and in seconds, I feel weightless.

"That's not possible. She's standing right here." Sam says as he turns around.

I can see the despair in his eyes as he looks all around the room frantically. Looking left and right, looking everywhere but finding nothing. He is alone, in an empty room. I am no longer visible to him. The phone starts to slide down his shoulder and to the floor. I can hear the man on the other end saying 'Sir', repeatedly. Sam's face fills with overbearing pain as he drops to the ground and stifles a cry. The lines around his lips and eyes become deeper than I have ever seen. I run over hoping to comfort him, but I know I cannot. It's too late. I am nothing but air now.

I reach out my hand and lay it on his arm, not able to feel his skin beneath mine. Knowing we need each other like our bodies need air but the air is gone. A tear escapes as I watch Sam sit on the floor and his body shakes from his suppressed sobs.

He looks at the spot where my hand now rests on his skin. "I'm so sorry."

He looks around the room desperately before he places his head in his hands with the tips of his fingers tangled in his half-damp hair.

I feel my body getting heavier once more. I place my free hand on his cheek. "I love you," I whisper as the dark surrounds me.

The Here After

Jane

I open my eyes and squint against the blinding white light that surrounds me. "Hello." Where am I?

No one answers.

I take a cautious step forward. A hand comes down on my shoulder and I jump around to see a woman who looks to be in her late sixties smiling at me.

"Hello, Jane."

"Hello," I reply shakily.

"My name is Edith. I'm here to be your guide."

While trying to clear the cobwebs of today's events, I take in the woman standing in front of me. She's around 5'6 in height and she's a little round in the middle. Her gray and white hair is neatly pinned up in a bun that rests high at the top of her head and her eyes are a beautiful gray, almost matching her hair.

"I trust your trip was pleasant."

Dumbfounded, I reply. "If you call dying pleasant."

"That is not what I meant, honey. Sadly, death finds us all in time."

"Well, I never thought it would find me so soon."

She smiles at me apologetically. "None of us do."

"I keep telling myself to wake up."

"That's normal, dear."

I look at her questioningly. "When does it finally sink in?"

"Depends on the person."

"Worst case scenario."

She looks at me sadly. "Some are still in denial." She takes my hand lightly and starts to move us forward. "But don't worry. We won't let you be one of those people. We want everyone here to find peace. After all, that's what it is about in the end. Peace. Acceptance. Understanding."

"What about Sam?"

She turns to face me, and I can see the surprise on her face. "What about him, dear?"

"I need to know he's alright."

"You need to focus on your journey now."

I stop and she stops with me. "I can't, not until I know he's going to be ok."

I can see in her eyes that she knows I am serious. I can't and won't focus on what I need or where I'm supposed to go from here, not until I can make sure he can move on. She talks about peace but how can I find peace knowing he has none?

She pats my hand lightly in understanding. "There may be a way. Come with me. There are a few things we need to take care of first."

Reluctantly, I allow her to lead us to our destination.

* * *

"Jacob, this is Jane, our newest member."

"Hello," Jacob says as he offers me his hand.

11

I reach out and take it and the first thing I notice is how soft it is. I look at our hands interlocked for longer than I should. I peer up into his dark chocolate eyes and I immediately regret it. Something about him feels familiar to me. His hair is short and sandy blonde in color. He must be around 5'6 in height, not much taller than I am. He can't be much older than twenty-eight from the look of him. This only gets me thinking about how many people die way before they should.

Edith's voice pulls me back and I quickly pull my hand away from Jacob which warrants me a look of hurt in his eyes.

"I'm sorry, what did you say?" I turn to Edith.

"I was asking if you were ready to move forward?"

"As long as where we are going involves seeing Sam."

Out of the corner of my eye, I can see a confused look on Jacob's face as he turns to Edith and asks, "Who's Sam?"

She smiles in his direction. "That was the name of her husband."

"Is he here as well?"

She shakes her head. "No. He is still alive."

"Then why-"

Edith cuts him off. "We will get there soon but first I want to show you where you will be staying."

I close my eyes and sigh. "Fine."

We start to walk away as I hear Jacob yell after us. "It was nice to meet you."

I follow Edith without another word.

Within a few minutes we reach what I am to assume is our destination. I look around the room and when I look up, I notice that there is no ceiling in sight. Everything is so white that I can barely make out any walls. The only thing I can see clearly are shelves and shelves of what seem to be files of some kind.

"Edith, what is this place?"

"This is the hall of records."

I gaze at her, confused.

She laughs. "This is where you can find a file on everyone living and dead." She points to the far-left corner, "Over there is a file on everyone still living."

She turns to her right and points, "And over there are all the files on everyone who has passed. The right side are the files on each person here."

"And the other section?" I ask about the area with files off behind us.

She looks at me sadly. "They have gone on to someplace I pray we will never see."

I swallow involuntarily. "So, the people who are still alive."

She looks over at me waiting for my question patiently.

"Do the files happen to say when or how someone is going to die?"

She nods.

"So, you can look anyone up and see that information?"

She nods again. "Now don't go getting any ideas. Even if you found the person you were looking for before someone stopped you, you have no way of contacting anyone. You're dead, remember?"

I look away sadly as I nod at her. Before anyone stopped me. I guess that means it is off-limits.

"You used up your one-time contact."

I look back at her in curiosity. "What does that mean?"

"When you went back to your home to see your husband one more time and talk with him. That was your one freebie."

For the first time since I arrived, I can feel the wheels turning in my mind. "Is there a way to get more?"

"You don't want to go there. Speaking to someone after you are already dead, takes a toll, not only on you but more importantly on them. They are the ones left behind, they need to pick up the pieces, move on, and keep living. If you care about them, you will let them do that and move on. You both need to find peace and you can't do that when you continue to live in the past. Living for something who is no longer here, no longer in reach, something you can't have, it's not healthy. Plus, you will be reunited one day. Until then you have to find a way to live without them."

"But what if he needs me?"

She looks over at the records of the living. "Who are we to say what they need?"

"I know Sam better than anyone."

"Not better than the person who created him."

I look at her surprised. "You mean?"

She nods.

"I always wondered if he was real. I believed but I never really knew where I would end up or if that was something I would never get an answer to. Even in death."

"Most people think the same."

She starts to walk away, and I follow her like a lost puppy. "So."

She looks over her shoulder at me. "Yes."

I sigh. "How do I get more freebies as you called it?"

She faces forward. "Like I said, I wouldn't suggest it."

"I didn't ask you that."

She stops and turns around to face me. "You are a stubborn one, aren't you?"

I smile sheepishly as I shrug my shoulders. "Sorry."

"Nothing comes for free and there is always a risk."

"I'm willing to take the risk."

She sighs. "And you are willing to let Sam go through all the pain of losing you all over again? Because that's what will happen." She turns forward again and starts walking. "I would think long and hard before you walk down this path. As I have said, it is best to let him find his path without you, and he needs to walk that alone. Being in contact even if it's a simple dream reminds them of what they have lost and only makes the process start all over for most people left behind."

I start to follow her and before I get the chance to say anything more a young woman walks up to us and hands her a file. "The file you asked for," she pauses and looks over at me and then lowers her voice before she continues, "about the person we talked about earlier."

Edith nods at her and the girl walks away. She tucks the file under her arm and ushers me forward.

"How far is this place?" I ask.

"Right around the corner."

"And this is where I'll be staying?"

She smiles. "It's where you will rest your head. But you can go anywhere you want to. Sky's the limit." She starts to giggle but it takes me a second to register the joke myself, but once I do I smile. "Oh, and before I forget Jacob will be here in a few hours."

"Why?"

"He will be your guide."

I look at her confused. "I thought that's what you were?"

She chuckles. "No, sweetheart, I was more of your, what would you call it? Your greeter. Since you have no loved ones here to greet you, I took on that role."

She stops in front of a door. "He will be here for you every day to check in until he's one hundred percent sure you're comfortable here."

I can hear the nervousness in my voice when I ask. "How long does that normally take?"

"Well, on earth it would be about a year for most people."

Afraid of the answer I ask, "And for us?"

She looks at me sadly. "Some people never get comfortable. They are in denial, or they feel cheated, like it was way before their time." She pushes the door open and walks inside. "You have clothes in the bureau. I suggest you get ready because he will be here soon."

I glance at her as confusion takes over my features. "He."

She looks at me concerned. "Jacob."

I laugh. "Oh, yeah. Sorry, I forgot."

"Is there anything else you need?"

I smile at her. "No, thank you."

She turns to walk out but before she does, she looks over her shoulder at me. "Jane, just remember what we talked about. Sam deserves to grieve you once, like normal people do. And I know right now you feel cheated, but keep in mind you are not the only one to die young. Some here are even younger than you. There is always a reason. God's will is never a bad thing. Try to remember that."

I can feel a tug of pain in my heart but before I get the chance to reply, she is out the door.

15

STAGE ONE:

<u>Denial</u>

Sam

"Sorry, to be the one to inform you."
"We did all we could."
I look behind me.
Jane?
She is gone.
"Sir."
The phone slides from my hand, down my leg and crashes to the floor.
My legs give out.
I crumble.
"Sir."
She's gone.
She can't be gone. I'm dreaming, that's it. I need to wake up.
I look around the room frantically.
Searching for her.
Any sign of her.
Nothing.

How is this possible? I was just talking with her. She was just telling me...telling me she came to say goodbye.

No. It's not possible. She is not gone. She can't be. She is only twenty-three years old and healthy, so healthy.

I feel a light chill on my right arm. I look down at it and find nothing there. I whisper, "I'm so sorry."

I say the words knowing I'm speaking to no one, that she can't hear me but needing to say the words, nonetheless. I should have believed her, should have done something. I look around the room in desperation. I can feel it creeping up on me, taking over my senses, searching, in need of something that's no longer there.

I feel the hopelessness engulf me as it swallows me whole and I place my head in my hands, the tips of my fingers pulling at my damp hair in desperation. I sit in this position for what feels like an eternity until something hits me.

Her cell phone.

I lift my head, eyes running wild over the floor, searching, until I see it. I pick up the phone in a feverish haste and start to dial Jane's cell phone. Just when I think the ringing will never end, I hear a click.

"Hello." Answers a shaky voice. Not Jane's.

I feel my heart coming to life in my chest. "Jane?"

The person on the other end hesitates and then clears her voice before answering. "I'm sorry. Is this Sam?"

"Yes." The word almost chokes me as it exits my mouth. "I'm looking for Jane."

I can hear her holding back a sob. "I'm so sorry. I thought someone had already called you."

Ignoring her I continue. "Can I please speak with her? It will only take a moment."

"She's... I... She's gone, sir."

"When will she be back?"

"She's not coming back, sir. She's dead. She died."

I smile. "No. See, that was a misunderstanding. That wasn't my wife."

"Sir, I know Jane. I saw her come in this morning. She looked…off. We were working on the same floor together when I saw her…she collapsed at the end of the hall. I was the one to retrieve the doctor."

I scream, "No!" I compose myself before I speak again, softer, "No, you have her confused with someone else."

"Sam, why don't you come down here and we will see what we can do to help?"

Click.

Not wanting to hear another word I drop the phone back on the ground at my feet.

"No." I close my eyes as I take a fistful of my hair and throw my head back till it connects with the hard cabinets. "I need to wake up." I open my eyes and look to the heavens as I yell. "You hear me! I need to wake up!"

Getting Adjusted

Jane

After Edith makes her exit, I look around at the room I will now be spending most of my time in. Just like everything else here, it's all white; white walls, white bed, white furniture. White, white, white, and white, everywhere I look. And for the first time, I feel trapped. I walk over to the ten-foot-high wardrobe and open the doors. Inside there are clothes folded and laying on the bottom shelf as well as hanging on hangers. To my surprise, they don't match the color of my walls and the rest of my room. I pick a maroon shirt from one of the hangers and a blue pair of jeans from below and close the doors. I walk over to the bed and throw them down in front of me.

These are my clothes.

How did they get my clothes?

Knock. Knock.

I turn my attention to the door. "Who is it?"

"Jacob."

"I'm getting changed. I'll be there in a minute."

"Take your time."

I look down at my clothes, staring at me from the bed. With a sigh, I lift my shirt up over my head and throw it down with an angry force before bending down to pick up my new one. I shove my arms through the holes and lift it over my head. I continue the process with my pants.

I make my way across my room until I am standing behind my door like a statue. I shake my head from side to side trying to clear the cobwebs that are forming in my mind. I place my hand on the doorknob and swing it open. On the other side is Jacob and he's smiling so wide that his canine teeth are showing.

"Hey, you ready?"

I look up into Jacob's deep Hershey-colored eyes and nod. His smile grows as he offers me his hand and I take it without a moment's hesitation. A second later he's pulling me down the hallway.

* * *

"So, what would you like to see first?"

As we make our way down the hall, I take notice of all the white doors, hundreds of them. There are at least ten different hallways we can go down and each one is lined with the doors on both sides.

How am I supposed to know which one to check out first?

I turn my gaze on him and without thinking I say. "I would like to know more about the freebies Edith was telling me about. I would like to know how I can go back, how I can help my husband."

He looks at me with a confused expression on his face, but I can see the understanding of what I am asking hidden deep in his eyes, "What do you mean going back?"

"Edith mentioned something about there being a way. Not in so many words, but I got the idea that there was a way to at least interact or talk with someone left," I pause trying to figure out the right word, "behind." I finish with a whisper.

"Well, you're not the first person to inquire about it, but I think we should get you more acquainted around here first and then we can talk more about that. How's that sound?"

Not good enough, "Reasonable."

He chuckles. "Good." He looks around at the different hallways before asking, "So, which path will we take first?"

"Which one would you suggest?"

A look of surprise inhabits his face. "No one's ever asked me that before."

"Well, it's not the first time I've been known to be different."

"And why doesn't that surprise me?" He says with a chuckle.

"Why?" I pause, unsure how to word my question but also afraid to ask it. "Why do I feel different?"

He looks at me with a puzzled expression. "What do you mean?"

"Like, I don't feel like myself."

"How so?"

I look down one of the halls. "I find myself thinking of Sam less than I know I would, among other things."

I look back at Jacob to see a reassuring smile on his face. "Sometimes people feel that way when they first arrive. It is a way of helping you cope. To make your passing easier. It allows you to settle and to accept that the life you lived, and knew for the years you were alive on earth, are no longer who you are."

"Well, I don't like it. I want it to stop." I look at him as I feel the fire in my eyes grow. "How do I get it to stop?"

His smile disappears. "I am not sure you can."

"There has to be a way. This is not what I would ask for and it isn't what I want. I want to feel lost, lonely and miserable. I want to feel like I was ripped out of my life early. I want to know what I'm feeling are my feelings, and not what someone is wanting or making me feel."

"I can understand that. It's just the way it's meant to be. All you have is peace, love, and your memories. Things are meant to be easier, but there is nothing easy about grief." He looks lost in thought for a moment before continuing, "How about this: we get you more acquainted with your surroundings today, and I promise that by tomorrow when we meet, I will have some kind of answers for you

I give him a questioning look. "You promise?"

"I promise." He says with a nod.

"Ok, then. Where to?"

His smile returns. "Well, I think we should check out the memory wing first."

"Huh?"

"Long story short, when you die things can be a little confusing or overwhelming and sometimes, we don't have our facts or memories straight, and because of that, it can be harder to start over."

I look down one of the hallways. "So, you want me to do what? Relive my memories?"

"In a word, yes."

"And you think this will make a difference?"

He nods his head.

"Then I guess let us give it a shot. I have nothing left to lose, right?"

* * *

The memories fly past me in a whirlwind of images. I hear Jacob's voice in the distance telling me to calm my heart rate and focus. I stifle a hysterical laugh.

Heart rate.

I am dead.

I close my eyes trying to remember something simple, early in life.

Then time stops. Or at least that is how it feels. The images come to a tortoise crawl as they spread out in front of me, passing ever so slowly. Each one begins to play out a scene, almost like I am watching a movie. One passes next to my face, the familiarity of it is comforting.

A little girl, no older than six in age, in a blue jumper and blue hat with flowers on it is running around a yard smiling, happy. I reach for the image, but it moves, and another takes its place. Before I can pull my hand back it connects with the image in front of me. It's Sam.

"I'm sorry the movie was so lame." Sam's voice is serene.

"No, I enjoyed it."

He chuckles, "You're too kind. But I don't need you to spare me. I know this was a horrible date."

I smile at him as I take his wrist in my hand lightly making us come to a stop. "No, really. I had a nice time. It wouldn't have mattered what we did."

His eyes sparkle at me in the night. "Really? But what if I took you to a zoo?" He smiles.

"After I ignored the fact that the animals were all in cages, I would still have a good time."

His smile disappears and it is replaced with a questioning look. "But, why?"

"Because of you, silly. As long as I'm with you, I'm happy."

His smile returns quickly. "Really?"

I chuckle. "Yes. I like being with you."

"And I, with you."

"Good."

"Jane."

"Yes?"

He takes my hands in his. "I would very much like to...try something."

I look at him in confusion but before I can ask what he is referring to he leans down, and his lips lightly touch mine. At first, a chill runs over my body sending the hair on my arms reaching for the heavens, but then a warmth takes over. I am calm, but more than that, I feel at home and safe as Sam's arms lightly wrap around my back. For the first time, I feel like nothing in the world can hurt me, not if I have Sam.

"You OK?"

The memory ends and I am back staring at the movie clip in front of my eyes in bewilderment. I feel a hand on my shoulder, and Jacob comes into view. He smiles at me reassuringly. It was then that I realized he asked me a question.

"Yes...I'm...I'm fine."

"The first one is always the hardest."

I look back at the images all around me. "I..."

"Maybe that's enough for today."

I glance at him in astonishment. "No, really I'm fine."

He smiles at me reassuringly. "Sometimes all you need is the one."

"What do you mean?"

"Some people here relive one memory and later that night the rest comes flooding back to them. Then they can start the next process."

"Process?"

He nods. "To peace."

I look away from him. "But what if they don't want peace?"

In a surprised tone, he asks. "Who wouldn't want peace?"

"What I mean is, what if peace isn't something they can obtain?"

He smiles at me lightly. "Everyone can find it, as long as they want it. But first, they must take the steps to lead to it."

"I don't see peace in my near future."

"And why is that?"

I look at him hoping he will understand what he is seeing in my eyes. "Because until I know Sam is OK until I know he is at peace, there is no hope in me finding it for myself."

STAGE TWO:

Anger

Sam

I stare at the phone in disbelief. I must be dreaming. Jane was just here. I can still smell her in the atmosphere around me, lavender. This isn't possible. I feel the fire bubbling in my stomach, fighting to come to the surface, to devour me. How could she be here with me one moment, and gone the next? We had our whole lives planned; we should have had fifty more years together before this was a reality for one of us.

Kids.

Family vacations.

Growing old together.

All of that is gone. It has all been ripped away from us. Taken without any warning. How is that fair? I look at the ceiling once more, but I don't see the white wall. I see what's beyond it, the sky, the heavens. I feel the heat like flames consuming me from the inside out. The anger is coming and there is no end in sight.

Anger.

Hate.

Loneliness.

That is all I feel. Bubbling to the surface, threatening the life I have built here, built with Jane. But there is nothing left to threaten. She's gone, our lives together extinguished like a flame denied oxygen, and there's nothing I can do to change it. Nothing I can do to bring her back home to me. There isn't a simple fix. It's not a night in the hospital after a car accident. Not a husband and wife arguing that leads to a night on the couch, a night of separation. This isn't something I can try to fight or be there for, not cancer, something that if you're lucky, goes away and becomes a distant memory after time. This is permanent. Something unchanging. Something no one can stop, no one can fight, no matter how hard they try or how badly they may wish to.

The darkness of my rage engulfs me like a brutish bear hug. I welcome it. It's the only thing keeping the hurt, the emptiness, at bay.

I'm not ready to think about her gone, gone forever. I feel the loss, the absence of her as my heart skips a beat and I shove the feeling away, not ready to let it in, let it consume me.

I ask you, what good is God, faith if this is where it takes you? Where is God now? Why did He take her from me? Why am I set in this life, destined to live it without her by my side? Why are the good the ones who suffer most in this thing we call life? We are born to go to school, work, love, grow, and die. Life has never been known to be easy or fair, but this is outside the norm. There's no answer for this; no answer to finding that one person to love and be lucky enough that they love you in return, to only lose them before your life together has even begun. Why? Why did this happen to us?

"Well, answer me!" I scream to the heavens. "What good are you if you couldn't prevent this? What is the purpose of your grand design in taking my wife, my love, my heart, my life? Answer me, damn it!"

I reach for the phone and close my hand forcefully around the hard plastic until my knuckles turn white. I pull my arm back and throw the phone with as much strength as I can across the room. It hits the front door and shatters into pieces. Chunks of black plastic scatter all over the tile floor. I look on at the pieces reminding me of my shattered heart, my shattered life, a life without my Jane.

First Step Towards Peace

Jane

Jacob was right about one thing; it wasn't an easy first night. My memories came flooding back to me in a demanding fashion as I slept. The hardest ones to relive were anything to do with my parents and Sam. They felt like I was reliving them all over again, in this moment, not like they were something I experienced years ago. Everything is so fresh now, on the surface of my mind and it's making this experience a little harder than it already was. I find myself thinking about my parents for the first time. How they didn't cross my mind sooner still evades me. I'm thankful that Sam will at least have them and they have him, as well as my sisters. I know they are going to need each other more than ever.

I never knew what loss felt like. I've had friends bury parents, friends, siblings, and more but I have never been on that end of the spectrum. I don't know what it's like to be the one left behind when someone leaves. However, now I know what it's like to be the one who left, to have no control over it, to want to go back more than you want to breathe. Dying is hard, but I have no doubt in my mind that living is harder.

* * *

"Fancy seeing you here?" I say as I approach Jacob from behind.

He turns around with a smile on his face. "Well, I knew you would come and find me once you were up to it today." He faces forward addressing the two young girls and the young man standing with him. "We can continue this conversation later."

The group looks over at me as I approach and just like everyone else here, they are smiling. Why is everyone always so happy?

Jacob turns his attention towards me, "How did you sleep?"

"I could lie and tell you great but I'm pretty sure you would see right through it."

His shoulders shake with the laugh that escapes his mouth. "I always say it's better to be honest, no matter what." He stops laughing as he places a reassuring hand on my shoulder, "but I am sorry you didn't have a first good night here. Hopefully, we can change the outcome for tonight. Peace is the end goal; remember that."

"I think we can make tonight a better one."

The face he makes shows me he knows where the conversation is about to go. He rustles the hair at the back of his head. "Jane, I..."

Not ready to be told I still can't see Sam today I cut him off, "What's on the agenda for today?"

He returns his hand to his side, "Jane, I think we need to talk more about this."

I wave his words off with a hand. "I don't want to hear it right now."

"Jane. You need to understand."

I turn on him hard and fast. "Understand what? That I am dead, that Sam's all alone and hurting, hurting worse than I am, and that you are telling me there's nothing I can do to help him? You wish to make me understand that?"

The look of shock on his face made me realize I had been yelling and had somehow come to stand on my tiptoes, like being taller would make him understand me better. I sheepishly lower myself until my feet are flat on the ground. I can sense everyone in the room looking in our direction as I place my hand on my elbow and fire forms under my cheeks.

"I'm sorry. I didn't mean to; I shouldn't have yelled at you."

"You don't need to apologize."

I look at him shyly, "Yes, I do."

"You seem to forget; I've been in your shoes. I understand how you're feeling and how frustrating it can be."

"I don't think frustrating covers what I'm feeling."

He shakes his head lightly, "No, it doesn't. However, I want you to know that what you are feeling is normal and it's a part of the process and no one here is going to begrudge you those feelings or your outbursts because I'm sure there will be more to come."

I looked at him in hope, "Did you have any?"

"Any what?"

"Outbursts."

His smile reaches the lines of his eyes, "Oh, many."

Surprised, I replied, "Really?"

"More than I care to admit actually."

I look down at my hands, afraid to ask my new question. "How long did it take you?"

He looks at me with a confused look on his face.

"To find peace, I mean. How long before you did?"

"Longer than I hoped it would."

"Well, at least you're honest."

He smiles at me sadly, "Like I said, it's always better to be honest."

"Yes. It is."

"Jane. You do need to try to come to terms with what's happened. I know it's not easy, but God never intended for death to be a sad or painful thing. It's meant to be happy. We are in our final resting place, a place of happiness and peace. That's all this is meant to be for you. However, until you accept it and learn to let the healing in, things won't get easier for you and this place isn't built for pain or grief. It's a place we've waited to reach since the moment we were conceived; a place of final rest. All our loved ones will be returned to us here when it is their time. That's something you need to hold onto."

"Jacob. I need to see Sam."

He looks away from me as he releases a sigh, "I know you do."

"Does that mean…?"

"I will see what I can do."

Without thinking I throw my arms around him and whisper, "Thank you."

I hear him whisper into my hair, "You're welcome."

* * *

Jacob walked me back to my room and told me he would return in a few hours. He said he needed to go talk to the higher-ups about my situation and see what he was allowed to show me before he did. Heaven is not what I would have expected, but I guess it makes sense that there are rules. How else would things be organized and how would anyone find peace? On earth there is always a way to do things and to get the results you want, but you need to put in the work. I'm trying so hard to fall in line and to do what is expected of me but it's hard knowing that Sam is by himself and feeling what I'm feeling, only worse.

Edith had mentioned how when we die, things shift for us in a way that is beyond our control and that it was designed that way to make the process of coming home, to our final resting place, easier. God wants us to find peace here. To do so, there are rules, or maybe I should call them guidelines, to follow. Life is hard enough to live and death is meant to be easier. The end of the road.

Part of me wonders if this is just the first stop. Like purgatory, but not really. More like we passed purgatory and made a pit stop before arriving at our destination. We come here first to prepare ourselves for what awaits us.

Here is where we go to decompress and let go of all the things that our lives back on earth held. Here we learn how to let go of the people and things that were in our lives so that we can move on and into peace.

"Would make sense, I guess."

I sigh as I glance back down at the book in my hands; one of my favorites from back home, *Clockwork Prince*. It is devastatingly beautiful in its own way; it always made me cry but somehow it was always reassuring. I think about the characters and how tragic their story was, but the journey was so breathtakingly beautiful to read, and I enjoyed every step. Suddenly my mind is overtaken with thoughts of Sam.

I drop the book as my hands fly to my head, pounding so hard I hold back a moan. I gasp as I throw my head back, eyes stinging.

"Sam."

I look straight ahead, pressure forming behind my eyes. In front of me, the picture starts to change, morph into something like a TV screen. A picture starts to form slowly. I suck in a fast breath when I realize what I'm looking at. It's my house, our room, and asleep on the bed is Sam.

I look on at him as my eyes start to tear up and moisture stains the skin of my cheeks. Sam starts to stir, and I strain to hear him say one word, one that makes my heart skip a beat and the tears rush down my face in a waterfall. I can hear the question, the longing in the word as he speaks it, and it breaks my heart.

"Jane."

STAGE THREE:

Bargaining

Sam

Slowly, I make my way up the spiral staircase to my bedroom, our bedroom. I sigh as I push open the door with the little strength I have left. Last night I slept on the couch. I couldn't find it in myself to make it up the stairs. However, why would I want to? Everything up here reminds me of Jane. Who am I kidding? Everything in my life reminds me of her and her absence. I thought sleeping downstairs would make it easier to wrap my head around her being gone and my new reality, but it didn't. As I closed my eyes, I prayed, silently hoping that I was only dreaming and that when I drifted off, I would return to my reality and Jane would be there shaking me awake as I slept through yet another alarm, just like I had dreamt last night.

"Babe, time to get up."

I roll over on my side with a groan as her giggle makes its way to my sleepy body.

"Babe, I need to get to work and if you don't get up now, you're going to be late getting to the restaurant."

"They can manage without me."

"I know, you trained Monica well, however, you know she prefers for you to be there in the mornings at least if nothing else."

I hear her moving things around on the chair next to my side of the bed. I roll over fast and grab her around the waist.

She sucks in a fast breath as I pull her back into bed and rest her back against my chest.

"Come back to bed."

"You know I can't."

I smile at her devilishly. "I think they can survive one day without you. Call in sick."

"Don't tempt me."

I place my hand on her neck and lightly pull her in for a kiss, her lips warm against mine. She runs her fingers through my hair as she parts our lips and rests her forehead against mine with a sigh.

"I need to go."

I grab at her hand. "How about we both call out today and stay in bed?"

"Whatever for?"

My grin spreads across my face as she returns a smile. "Why, else? Let's work on that baby we've been talking about."

"Sam." She blushes.

"Jane," I say in a playful tone. "But seriously, we've been talking about kids for a while now. Do you still want a baby?"

"Of course, and I have faith that when the time is right, God will bless us with one. Right now, well, it is just not our time."

Wanting to make light of a now kind of serious topic I grab her around the waist once more as she screams playfully as I begin to tickle her.

Then I woke up.

Sweating.

Nervous.

Frantic.

And alone.

It was only a dream, a happiness I could no longer have. I sigh as I take my first step into our cold, dark room. I stare at our unmade bed, recalling yesterday's events. Hearing someone come in the front door and forgetting all about making the bed before I descended the stairs to find that the intruder was no one other than my Jane.

I walk over to my dresser, one that Jane picked out for me. I open the top drawer to retrieve my socks and boxers, close it, and open the next for my shirt, then repeat the process until I have my new clothes in hand. I stare at them in a daze.

I need a shower.

I know I do.

I move towards the bathroom and place my clean clothes on the sink counter. I slide the shower door open and turn the water on hot, full blast. I pull my shirt over my head in a trance and discard it to the floor at my feet.

I pause.

I stare at the water.

Listen as it beats on the shower floor.

Listening.

Stuck.

Frozen.

I can't. I don't have the drive to enter the shower, to let the water wash over me in a calming warmth, to release my anger, my fears, to clean yesterday from my body, and my mind. I can't.

Without another thought, I turn away from the running water and make my way to our bed. I look down at the welcoming gray sheets and comforter. Before I realize what I'm doing, my body hits the bed hard. I grab for the closest pillow and pull it in close for a hug. I breathe in.

Lavender.

Jane.

I feel the pressure forming behind my eyes, pain. My vision turns blurry as my eyes rest on a picture of Jane and me in the Caribbean, where we spent our honeymoon. I close my eyes in haste as the tears make their way to the surface once more. I grip the pillow tight as my legs move in towards my body and I lay there in the fetal position fighting back the tears once more while trying to hold the pieces of my heart together.

As a man, I never thought this was something I could feel. I've felt pain in the past but nothing like this; broken, empty, alone. I can't hide this.

In the other room, I can hear the water still running; a reminder of how far I've fallen, how lost I feel, and how the broken pieces inside of me will never heal.

* * *

"Jane."

With the heaviness of sleep, I reach over and touch the cold open spot on the bed next to me, empty. Groggily I pry my eyes open, blurry. I gaze about the room trying to recall how I got here. What's that noise? It's coming from the bathroom. Water? I move slowly into a sitting position and rub my eyes feverishly, uncertain. I stand, finding my legs still wobbly from sleep, placing one foot in front of the other slowly until I make it to the bathroom. I push the door open as a hot fog hits me square in the face and takes my breath away. I reach the shower, throw open the door, and turn the nozzle off. I look down at my feet to see one of my onyx-colored short-sleeved shirts.

I feel my eyebrows meeting in the middle of my face as I raise a hand to meet them, staring at the object in question confusingly. I bend over, reaching for the discarded garment alone on the damp moisture-covered tile floor. My hand takes in a fistful of cotton as the fog departs from my brain. I fell asleep, I was going to take a shower but then. *Jane.* I close my eyes at the painful thought as my memories of the last two days pull me back to my new reality.

I hear the doorbell ring. My eyes fly open. I lift the cotton material over my head, shoulders, and back into place. Sluggishly, I descend the stairs. I pause. Take in a slow breath and open the door.

There, in front of me stands Monica, shoulder length fawn hair resting lightly against her maroon shirt. Her emerald-painted nails draw my attention, hands intertwined. She turns to look me in the eyes with a smile that shows her teeth only a little as her jade eyes shine in the late morning sunshine.

The restaurant.

"Monica, I'm so sorry I... I should have called."

She looks at me startled as her smile disappears from her face, "Sam, what's wrong?"

"I." I don't know how to say the words. I can't form them, they are getting stuck in my throat, and I'm choking on them.

She lightly places her hand on my arm. "Sam?"

"It's Jane." The words come out in a whisper.

"Is she alright?"

I can only shake my head.

"Sam, talk to me."

"She's..."

She waits patiently.

The pain returns to my eyes, but I fight it back. "She's."

I can't get it out.

Softly Monica asks. "She's what Sam?"

The words fly out of my mouth in a whirlwind as they collide with each other. "She's gone."

Puzzled, she asks, "Gone?"

I look away from her as the moisture wins the fight to the surface.

"What do you mean gone, Sam?"

I choke out the following words as my shoulders begin to shake violently. "She's dead."

"What! How? When?"

She reaches for me as I turn away, retreating into my stale home. "Yesterday." I pause unsure. I can't make sense of the time, or the day. What day is it today? Was it yesterday? Unsure, I say, "I think."

I walk to the kitchen leaving her alone at the door. I can feel her gaze lingering on me. I hear the door quietly clicking home. I sigh in relief. I'm alone once more. I don't wish to talk to anyone, don't want to think about it, not ready to admit she's gone. Then I hear it.

37

Footsteps.

She couldn't have, could she?

"Sam," she says my name gently, almost in a whisper, like she is addressing a spooked lion afraid it will pounce at any moment.

I push down the dark abyss fighting to take hold as I strongly ask, "Would you like something to drink?"

"Sam." She says it a little louder this time.

"Monica."

"Please, talk to me. What can I do? How can I help you?"

I reach into the cabinet and pull out a 16-ounce plastic cup. Jane preferred them over glass and always said less chance of breaking anything if nothing was glass. I smile at the thought. I place it down on the counter as I make my way to the fridge.

"We have water, tea, or cranberry juice." I turn to look at her for the first time. "Anything sound good?"

She only shakes her head.

I turn my attention back to the fridge and pull the cranberry juice from its cool home. Pouring the contents into my awaiting cup, I stare at the liquid hard as it leaves one home and enters another. A new and unfamiliar home. Lost in the moment, the thought, I catch myself just as the liquid reaches the top of my glass. I add the lid back to the container and return it to its home. The coolness reaches my lips, passes them and as it travels down my throat, the hairs on my arms stand up. The contents are cool and refreshing. I down the whole glass and discard it in the sink. I walk past Monica. She watches me silently as I make my way to the living room couch.

I hear her sigh lightly from the kitchen, then light footsteps.

She gestures with her hand to the empty spot next to me, "May I?"

I nod, she sits.

"Can I call your parents?"

"Please, don't. I don't need them coming here."

"Maybe they should. Sam, someone needs to help you with this, with the arrangements."

I turned to her. "I don't want to talk about it."

I can see the sadness for me in her eyes, plainly enough that my heart responds in my chest. "Please, maybe you should go."

"I can't leave you like this."

"I'm asking you to."

I can hear the stubbornness in her tone. "I won't."

In a pleading voice, I say, "Please, Monica."

She shakes her head. "No, I won't do it. After everything you and Jane," she pauses watching my reaction I suppose, "after everything you've done for me. I can't leave you, not like this. This feeling, it will swallow you whole if you let it and I won't let that happen to you."

I chuckle hard enough that my shoulders shake in jest. "You talk as if you know the feeling."

She whispers. "I do."

I glanced at her in surprise. "Who?"

She looks out the window. "My sister. I lost her when I was only fourteen years old. We were inseparable. I still feel the absence of her every day," she looks back at me, "but it is easier."

"I don't know how this, this emptiness, could get easier. I can barely separate dreams from reality. It doesn't feel real."

"That's also normal. I remember it took me a few weeks before things made sense again, or I should say before my new reality sunk in."

"I don't know if I'm strong enough to make it that long."

I feel her hand on my arm before I see it. "You are stronger than you think, and I'll be here to help as long as you want me and your parents."

I cut her off, "I don't want to call them."

"I think you should."

I stand so fast I startle her. "I'm not ready to deal, to talk about it; about a life without her and that's what they will try to get me to do."

"I understand, but the longer you deny what happened the harder it will be for you."

I know she's right, but I'm not ready. How will I ever be ready? We were only married eight short months ago, we were meant to have many years ahead of us. We were talking about children and our future more these last few weeks than ever before and now that's all gone. I have this crater-sized hole in my heart where she used to be, and I don't know how I am ever going to fill it.

What about Jane? Where is she? How is she? Can she feel? Is she sad? Can she see me?

"I can tell you're somewhere far away right now. Tell me what you're thinking about?"

"I was thinking about Jane. About where she is, how she's feeling."

She nods her head in understanding. "I still wonder the same thing about my sister and sadly, those are answers we won't get till our days are done here and we get to see them again, but I have to believe they are at peace."

I whisper, "Do you think she's still here?"

"Meaning?"

"Like, do you think she can still see me, even though I can't see her?"

She flashes me a reassuring smile. "I do. I believe even after they are gone, they still visit us and find ways to let us know they are still around."

"How?"

"Well, I remember a few times I would be thinking about her or crying, and then I would hear a song that reminded me of her or had some attachment to her. Sometimes, I would feel cold when it was warm only moments before. Other times I would be all alone and swear I would hear footsteps or a knock. There have been many different things over the years, and I believe it's her way of reassuring and comforting me."

"But if she moved on and was in heaven, how would she communicate with you still?"

She shrugs, "I'm not sure."

"Then how do you know?"

She raises a hand to her heart. "I can feel it here. I know she is at peace, but I also know she's still here with me. It's hard to explain."

"Do you believe in God? I know you believe in heaven but that doesn't always mean someone believes in God."

"Yes, I do." She states, matter-of-factly. "Do you?"

I look away from her, "I did."

"And now?"

"I don't understand, if there is a God, how he could do this. How could He take your sister from you at such a young age and now, Jane? They both had only begun to live. It seems almost cruel."

Monica looks down at her black high heels before speaking again. "I don't think it's God who does it."

"He made us, He created life, so He had to be the one to end it."

"Not necessarily. At least I don't think so."

"Then what do you believe?" I ask almost breathlessly.

"I believe God created us with a single purpose. Once that purpose is fulfilled, our journey is done and we are called home. I also believe in our free will and when it comes to that, we create paths that God never intended us to walk down and because of that, loss occurs. I believe many die before they get to achieve what they were meant to in this life."

I feel the anger mixing with uncertainty in my stomach as I ask, "But they were so young. How could they have achieved what they were sent here to do already?"

"Maybe they didn't."

"Then why did they die?"

She shakes her head unsure. "I don't have all the answers, Sam. I only know what I feel and believe in my heart. There is a reason for everything that happens in our lives. Each choice, each loss guides us down a different path in life."

I feel like I'm looking down an endless empty tunnel with no end in sight. "I don't know which path I'm meant to take now."

"You will in time. The important thing is not to lose yourself or your faith in the process of finding peace again."

"I think it's already too late for that."

"It's never too late."

Her words linger in the space between us for a moment longer than they should.

She glances at the door before saying, "You need to call your parents. It's already been a few days. There are things that need to be done and soon, things that are going to be too hard for you to deal with right now. I'll help with what I can but trust me, you will want them here for what's coming next."

I feel her gaze like a caress on my face as a flaming inferno builds in my stomach and rises to my heart. I can feel something other than anger, loneliness and uncertainty forming there; something darker. It's hatred, hatred for a God who has failed me, failed my wife. For twenty-six years I prayed, held true to my faith, to God. I believed in Him and what He represented until now.

I look out the window and to the heavens asking God how he could do this, as I feel the darkness surrounding my heart in a warmth I've never felt before. Desperately I implore Him, begging Him to fix this, to bring her back. I'll do anything you ask of me. I plead, but my words are, as always, unanswered. He's silent, as always, and I'm waiting for an answer that will never come.

Finding A Way

Jane

I watch everything in a trance, like a bad episode of my favorite show playing on the TV screen before my eyes. I see Sam get out of bed, and turn off the water that he must have left running the night before, I hear the doorbell ring, and see him go down the stairs and open the front door. I watch as Monica enters our home and tries to find the right words to say to him, to reassure and comfort him but just as clearly, I see how nothing she is doing is helping.

Then I hear it, hear him, in my head. I hear him talking, no, pleading, with God, asking him how he could do this and how he would do anything to bring me back, and then I feel him shut down. I feel the darkness overshadow him as if it were happening to me and then the picture fades into nothingness.

Oh, Sam.

I need to do something fast. His faith was the main thing that pulled me to him. I loved how brightly he shined with his devotion and love for God as well as his understanding. We grew together in our faith, and it was what made our relationship everything it was. Sam was, is, who he is because of his faith, and I fear the man he will become without it.

I need to find Jacob, I need to find a way to help Sam, now, before it is too late and he's too far gone. I reach for the doorknob but not before I turn to look once more at the place where I witnessed the events unfold. How did I do that? Without another thought, I turn the knob and head down the hall.

* * *

"Jacob."

"Hey, I was just coming to find you."

"I...I saw Sam." I blurt out before he reaches my side.

His pace slows as my words reach him, "You? How?"

I come to a stop, now in front of him. "I don't know how I did it. I was reading a book that reminded me of him and next thing I knew I was seeing him through something like a TV screen."

Jacob's hand meets his chin. "I've never heard of someone being able to do that on their second day here. Well, not really second, but still."

Confused, I forget about the topic for a moment. "It is my second day here."

He looks at me as a smile spreads across his features, "Oh, yes, but time moves differently here. It may be only two days in our time, two days and two nights, but back on earth time moves differently."

"What do you mean?"

"For example, come tomorrow, our tomorrow, it would have been a week on earth."

"How...why?"

Jacob starts walking forward, I follow suit. "I don't know. It's always been like that."

What purpose, what difference would it make at the end of the day to have time move differently here and there? It makes no sense to me. However, I have more important fish to fry. I turn to Jacob.

"Yesterday, when I asked you to look into a way to stop me from forgetting

Sam."

He cuts me off. "Oh, yes. I did find a way to help with that. Anytime you feel him slipping or things shifting, and you don't want them to, just focus harder on him and it will stop."

I scoff, "That simple, huh?"

"Seems to be, at least."

"Yeah, well hate to burst your bubble but I brought it up to let you know I already figured it out." I smile.

"Oh," he rubs at his neck in a feverish gesture, like he's embarrassed about something, "I guess you would have if you saw him."

"Speaking of which."

He glances down at me, "Yes."

"He's not doing so well."

He faces forward once more. "That's to be expected, I'm afraid. There are, after all, five stages of grief. I would be surprised if he made it through all five already. Most end up having to go through a few steps before their lives return to some form of what is normal. Most people stay stuck on at least one of the steps for a while."

"He's so lost, Jacob. I have to do something."

"I don't know if there is anything to be done."

"But you said."

He cuts me off apologetically. "I know what I said but it's really in both of your best interests if you do this on your own."

I shake my head back and forth forcefully. "I don't care how long it takes me, I'm talking about Sam, here."

He looks at me puzzled, "Even if it means prolonging you finding your own peace?"

"I don't care."

"Interesting."

Ignoring his response, I continued, "I left him. He had to stay and continue living, I didn't. I can't imagine how he's feeling, and I need to help him. He's losing who he was, he's losing his faith, what makes him Sam. I can't sit here and just let it happen, not if I can do something to help."

"If you're sure…"

I nod. "I am."

He nods in understanding. "Then there might be a way to let him know you are there watching him and that you want him to be happy. But it's not easy."

"Nothing worth it ever is."

His smile grows as he looks at me with amazement. "Never have there been truer words. However, I need you to remember by doing this, if it's not done right, you will cause more harm than good."

"Then we will make sure I do it right."

Unexpected Guests

Sam

Knock. Knock.

What now?

Monica left a few hours ago and I found myself surprisingly happy to return to the quiet. Not that I didn't appreciate her coming here or talking to me, but it wasn't helping. If anything, it was only making me angrier. At the end of our conversation, she told me she would check in with me tomorrow and told me not to worry about the restaurant, which honestly was the furthest thing from my mind. All the things that used to matter or make me happy hold less meaning for me now. I can't seem to get interested in even the smallest of things, like a shower.

The thought of Monica coming tomorrow to 'check in on me' unsettles me. Having someone look at you with sadness and pity and be a constant reminder of what is now missing from your life does not help anything. I know she means well but honestly, I would much rather be left alone to wallow, sit in my filth, be numb.

I reach out my right hand, feeling the chilly doorknob and I reluctantly turn it. The cold evening air hits me square in the face as it takes the wind from my lungs so fast that I choke. However, when I see who's behind my front door, that takes my breath away more than anything.

My parents.

How did they know?

"Mom. Dad. What are you…"?

My mother steps forward and throws her arms around me. This isn't her normal loving embrace. She's holding me tightly, almost as if she's trying to hold me together. Afraid to lose me too.

Through a light sob, she says into my chest, "I'm so sorry, my love. I'm so deeply sorry."

I look at my father for help, but I can see in his eyes, that he's just as lost as I feel, and I know the only thing I can expect from him are words, a lecture, reassurance. Things I don't want. Things I can't handle right now.

I find myself still forgetting that it happened, that she's gone. I don't need anyone here to remind me of it or to try to make it better. Nothing can make this better. This hole, this crater in my heart, it's here to stay.

My mother pulls back to look up at me with teary eyes and I feel my heart break a little more. My mother was the first woman I came to love, always there for me, always caring and knowing the right thing to say to fix whatever evil had entered my life, but I'm afraid she can't fix this. To see her like this, it's always been hard for me, for a woman so small yet so very strong. I can count on one hand how many times I've seen her cry and almost every time she's shed tears, they have been for me.

"Momma, what are you and Poppa doing here and so late in the day?"

She doesn't release me as she turns to my father, I've seen that look before, she's asking him for his assistance, knowing that her voice will betray her.

My father speaks. "We…we know what happened, son. We wanted–" He looks at my mother, who is still clinging to me like she's holding on for dear life. "We wanted to come and check on you."

I smile. "I'm fine. You made the drive for nothing." I look down at my mother, sorrow embedded in every line on her face. "But you should come in for a hot cup; it's a cool night."

I turn away and my mother's embrace ends, only for her to place her small, clammy, soft hand in my cool, scarred one. She gives it a light reassuring squeeze as we make our way inside. It's not until we reach the kitchen she finally, reluctantly, releases my hand.

I head over to the cabinets as I ask, "What would you like to drink?"

My father stumbles over his words as he answers, "Tea is fine, son."

I reach up and pull out three teacups and make my way over to the kettle. I begin filling it with water when I hear whispering behind me.

"You know I can hear you so you might as well speak up."

My father sighs, "Son, we really should sit and talk."

"We will, I just want to get the tea first."

I hear my mother take a step in my direction. "Sam."

"Yes." I continue filling the kettle, slowly, not wanting to have this conversation but knowing they aren't going to leave until we do.

"You're not acting."

She stops abruptly.

"Acting like what?" I question.

She hesitates before saying, "You're not acting like yourself. You're worrying me."

"Oh, is that all?"

I hear her suck in a breath behind me and I'm angry with myself. My mother has always been the best person I've ever known, and I would never intentionally hurt her. I know she's only here because she cares but right now, I don't want someone who cares. Right now, all I want is to be left alone. To figure out what to do next; how to live, how to breathe, how to continue with my life without my wife, my partner.

How could life have been so great only a few days ago and now I'm stuck in this recurring nightmare? When will it end? I know death is a part of life, but I never thought one of us would take that path until many years from now. We were both so healthy. None of it makes any sense. Even now, I feel like it's all a dream, that in a few short hours she will be walking through our front door again.

"Sam," My mother's voice reaches me from far away, pulling me back from a place of emptiness.

It's then that I feel the warm water running over the kettle and onto my hand. I turn off the water and place the object on the stove top and ignite the flame. I place my hands on the countertop and lean over, head down.

"I'm sorry, mom. I...I went away for a moment."

I felt her hand on my back, but I refused to turn around.

"Son, I can't begin to understand what you're going through, but I want to help. Please, let me."

"I don't think there is anything you can do to help, Mom."

"We won't know until you let us try."

I sigh, "It's too hard right now, Mom. Too fresh. I'm not ready."

My father speaks for the first time. "You can't wait to talk about this, Sam. The longer you do the worse off you'll be."

Anger flares up in my gut. I turn around to face him and before I can stop myself my voice comes out not my own. "What do you know about it? You still have Mom. You don't know a thing about what I'm going through."

A deeper sadness enters his eyes. "I won't begin to act like I do. But I know about loss, and I know it will eat you up if you let it."

"Then so be it."

My mother gasped next to me. For a moment I had forgotten she was even in the room. "Don't talk like that, Sam."

"I'm sorry, Mom, I. I don't have the fight in me to do more than what I'm doing right now, at this moment."

She places her hand on top of mine. "That's what we are here for."

"You don't need this."

"You're our son, your pain is our pain. Your loss is our loss. We loved Jane; she was our daughter. We will miss her deeply, but you are the one left behind, you are the one mourning and you are the one I'm concerned about."

"I wish you wouldn't be."

She smiles at me lightly, "A mother's love runs deep. There's nothing I wouldn't do for you. If I could take this on I would, only so you wouldn't have to."

"I know."

She places her hand lightly on my cheek. "Come, let's sit on the couch while we wait for the water to boil."

Reluctantly I followed her to the living room. My father gives me a wide berth as he sits on the couch furthest from the one my mother and I are occupying.

"I know you don't want to talk about it but there are things we need to know if we are going to help you." My mother's voice is almost a whisper. Almost as if she's afraid to wake the beast inside of me once more.

I close my eyes. "Like what?"

I open them to look at her and I can see she's fighting with herself. "I want to help with the arrangements. I don't want you to have to worry about them."

"Arrangements?"

My father's words come out softer than I've ever heard them in my life. "The funeral plans."

"Oh."

I feel all the air get sucked from my lungs like I've been hit in the gut with a ten-pound brick. The funeral.

My mother gently says, "We want to help. But without us knowing what, what you both had planned, it's hard for us to do much."

"I."

I'm frozen.

Not in fear.

Not in loneliness.

I'm frozen in the unknown.

"I. We didn't. I don't know."

She pats my hand lightly where it sits on my lap. "That's fine, son. We will figure it out."

My father's voice sounds foreign as it reaches my ears. "Did she have a will?"

"Um...I..."

She did, I remember now. Right after we got married, she insisted on us doing one. I told her she was crazy, and we were young, that nothing would happen to us. Boy was I wrong.

"Yes."

He nods in approval. "Good."

Good?

"You're going to need it."

"What for?"

He looks at me surprised. "What do you mean what for?"

My mother looks at him sternly. "Joshua, enough."

"I'm only trying to help."

"Well, stop."

He looks out the window. "As you wish, dear."

For the first time, I look at my father. I haven't seen him in a few months. Since Jane and I got married and bought the house and the restaurant, life took a whole new path. One that didn't allow me to see them as much as I would have liked.

My father looks much older today. The gray in his black hair is bright, almost white. The lines around his eyes and lips are deep and defined. The color is nearly drained from his eyes, looking almost white in color instead of the deep gray I am used to. Has time caught up to him so quickly?

Afraid to look at my mother, afraid to see the same changes in her, I look out the window opposite the one my father is staring out of.

My mother's voice washes over me in a warmth I've long since needed. "Do you remember where it is, son?"

Confused, I ask, "Where what is?"

Understanding and sorrow flash across her features, "The will, honey."

"Oh, uh, yeah it's in our room. In the top drawer of the dresser. Jane talked me into getting them done a few months ago."

My father whispers, "She was a smart girl."

Anger boils up inside my veins. "Don't talk about her like that."

Surprise embeds itself in my father's facial features. "Like what? I didn't- "

I cut him off. "In the past tense."

Realization hits him as his expression softens. "I didn't mean it like that." He looks me in the eyes sadly. "I'm sorry, Sam. I didn't mean it like it sounded."

The beast softens.

Unsure.

Unaware.

Unafraid.

It wants to come out, wants to be free. I won't let the beast out. I won't become that man. He's not someone I want to be, not someone Jane would be proud of, not someone she would love.

"I know you didn't, Dad. I'm sorry."

"No need."

I rub my eyes feverishly. "I'm not myself."

My mother speaks. "That's understandable."

I look at her, anger filling my heart, my mind, my veins. "It shouldn't be. I shouldn't be taking my anger out on you."

"Then who would you take it out on?"

I don't think. The word flies out of my mouth before I can stop it. "God." And I immediately regret it.

My father's body language changes completely. From soft, caring, and understanding to hard, rigid, and questioning.

"What do you mean, God?" He asks, not lovingly.

"I only meant…"

"No, boy, spit it out."

"Joshua."

He looks at my mother with loving eyes, but his voice doesn't match the softness. "Don't Joshua me."

"I meant nothing by it."

He turns on me, all the love that was there when he was looking at my mother, vanished. "No, what did you mean by that statement, Samuel."

Oh, man, I am in for it now. It's never a good thing when he uses my full name. "I only meant. He, well, He is to blame. He creates life and He ends it."

"Boy, you know nothing about our God, and remember nothing of what we taught you if that's what you think."

"Then I guess I know nothing."

"Don't you talk like that."

53

I find the beast waking in the darkness, wanting to come out and play. I try to push him back down. "Talk like what? It's the truth. I'm angry and I don't understand. How could a God who loves us sit back and watch as our lives become turmoil?"

My father is about to cut me a new pair, but my mother's look silences him. She is the one to speak. "Son, that isn't how it works, and you know that. God doesn't choose who lives and who dies. We make our own path in this life. No one goes without pain and suffering. If He could protect us from it, he would."

I cut her off. "How can you be so sure?"

"Because He is our father and being your mother, I know how a parent loves their child. We would do anything to protect them if we are able."

"But he's God. He could have stopped this."

"That's not in God's control. When it's our time to go, it's our time. And when we go, He is there to welcome us with open arms just as He is here now, walking beside you every step of the way along your grief."

"I know you mean well, Momma, but I don't think that's the case."

"Do you not remember the picture, the saying I had hanging in your room as a little boy?"

I look at her confused.

"The footsteps in the sand."

It comes back to me fast, taking me off guard, like waves hitting the sandy shore, fast and hard. "Oh, yes. The one with the beach and the two pairs of footprints in the sand, but then they turn into one."

She nods. "Yes. That is God, my dear boy. He walks beside you and when you can no longer walk, he picks you up. That is why the two pairs turn to one. For that is when you are at your lowest, that is when he carries you."

"Well, I'm sorry to say, Momma, but there has only been one pair this whole time and it's not because He's holding me."

I can see in her eyes she is feeling defeated.

"Momma, I'm sorry. I don't mean to hurt you. That's the last thing I want."

"It's not me you are hurting, son. It's you. You and God. How do you think this would make Jane feel?"

Her question takes me by surprise but more than that, I know she's right. The main thing Jane loved was that our faith was a mirror image of one another.

"I don't know, Momma. The only thing I know for sure is she's not here and if the roles were reversed, I'm certain she would be feeling the way I am now."

"I don't think she would."

I try to hide the tiredness from my voice. "And why is that?"

"I knew Jane well. Maybe better than you think."

"OK."

"The one thing that mattered most to her in this world was her faith. She loved you more than anything else, but her faith always came first. I have no doubt in my mind that she would be hurting and mourning and even angry. However, I also know that she wouldn't be blaming God or turning her back on Him for losing you."

"Maybe, maybe not."

"No maybe about it. She would turn to him for help. She wouldn't push him away; she would find peace in her faith."

"Jane was stronger than me, always has been. Better than me too. I'm not that strong, Momma. I wish I were, but all I am is angry. That's all I feel."

"I can understand that. I know God will too, once you've had time and find your way back."

I release a breath I've been holding. "I don't know if I will."

She sighs. "I just hate seeing you like this, grieving and angry, in the dark without our Lord and Savior. He can't come in if you don't let Him."

"I fear God has abandoned me. This is something I can't let go, can't overcome. Jane was the reason I became the man I was. She was what made my faith stronger. Without her, I'm a shell of that person. The person she loved."

She smiles. "You can still be that person if you wanted to."

"I don't know how to be without her. There is nothing left here." I place my hand over my heart, "She was my reason for being. She made this life bright and worth living and being the best version of myself for her."

"Talk to her. Ask her for guidance to lead you out of the darkness you are in."

"I'm not in the dark, Momma."

She looks at me sadly with tears forming in her eyes. "Oh, my dear boy, but you are. You are."

Reaching Out

Jane

"How does it work?"

Jacob looks at me unsure. "From what I gather, you think of someone hard enough and the portal will open again."

"I got that, but what do I do once it does?"

"That's the tricky part."

I roll my eyes, getting impatient.

"You have to focus on something in the picture, something you want to move or use to let them know you're there."

"Got it."

"Most people turn on the lights or change the radio station. Others can get in the person's mind and have them flip the station to one that is playing a song that will remind them of them."

"Wow, really?"

"Yeah. It normally takes a while to get that advanced though, and we try not to have people still in the mourning process. By that time, we hope everyone has found peace."

I grin. "Well, I'm a fast learner."

He chuckles, "Indeed, you are."

"I'm going for the gold."

Horror takes over his expression as I walk away. "Wait, what?"

"You heard me," I say with a smile over my shoulder.

"I don't think that's a very wise idea."

"No one ever said I was wise."

I can hear him starting to walk faster, trying to catch up with me. "Jane, you really should think about this."

"I have."

He places a hand on my shoulder ordering me to a halt. "I don't think you have."

"Jacob, Sam is out there alone. He's losing himself. He's turning on God. I need to do something drastic and fast."

He lifts his hand and runs it through his hair. "I don't think this is a good idea."

"Why not? I mean, what could go wrong?"

He returns his hand to his side. "I don't know, precisely."

"Exactly my point. Maybe nothing will happen, other than me reaching him."

I started walking again, back to my room, to where I felt closest to Sam since I arrived here.

"Jane."

I stop, frustration taking hold. "What?"

"Do you mind if I at least come with you?"

I'm sure the surprise is clear on my face when I reply. "Um, sure."

I turn and start walking again, Jacob on my heels.

"How do you plan on reaching him?"

"I think I'm going to try to get into his mind."

"And?"

I glance over at him. "I haven't gotten that far yet."

"Don't you think you should think this through a little more before jumping in with both feet?"

I shake my head. "There's no time. I told you."

"But what if you do more damage than good?"

I stop abruptly. "How could I do that?"

"If you go in and you don't show him something positive, something to let him know you're at peace and want him to find it as well, it could end badly."

"Noted." I continue walking.

"All I'm suggesting is to find something significant to both of you. Something he can't mistake for you reaching out to him. Find that first before you go jumping into the guy's head."

I hate to admit it, but what if he's right? I mean, he has been here longer than me. He's my guide for a reason, right? I don't want to do anything to set Sam back. I need him to move past this, past me. I need him to live again, to trust God again.

Lightbulb.

"I've got it."

I take off running leaving Jacob in the dust calling after me in frustration.

* * *

Jane

I feel the steam emerging from my ears.

My brain is on fire.

I'm killing my brain cells.

I laugh.

I'm dead. I don't need them anymore, right?

I ignore my inner thoughts, shaking my head free of them.

Focus, Jane.

The image starts to take shape in front of me. Colors, shapes, and then it molds into a clear picture. So clear it feels like I'm standing in the restaurant myself. I look around the room, searching, hoping.

There.

Across the room.

Monica.

I knew I needed to do something drastic, fast and the only person I could think of was Monica. We were close but not close enough for her to truly be mourning me and because of that, I know it's safe, safe to reach into her mind to tell her to go to Sam. Have her help him move on.

With her.

I know I'm crazy right? I only just died and I'm already trying to push another woman into my husband's arms. However, it's not like that. I know Monica. Her faith is just as strong as ours and I know if anyone can help Sam get through this, it's her.

I remember when she told me about losing her sister when she was younger, and I asked her how she handled it. She told me it was the hardest thing life had ever thrown at her and without the love of her family, she never would have found her way out of the dark abyss and to the surface again. Because of them, she was able to breathe once more, to find peace.

I could feel the loss in her still as we spoke of the tragic event that set Monica on her new path in life. However, I also saw a strong, God-loving woman. Someone who understood that God was not responsible for the hole that now took up residence in her chest. He was not responsible for the pain Monica felt, the tears that showered her cheeks. However, He was responsible for holding her up, helping her find her way back to peace. He was there in the people around her, the beauty in the lilies that reminded her of her sister. He was there holding her up, guiding her. He was in the ears of those around her, giving them inspiration, telling them what to say, what to do to help her heal.

God was always there.

He was the footsteps in the sand.

He was always next to her.

And when she felt she couldn't go on, He would carry her.

I needed her to remember this, remember what got her through and I needed her to help Sam find that same place of peace. I'm sure by now his parents are at our place and I know they mean well, but his father never knew the best way to handle Sam. I know he will try to get him to see that God isn't responsible and that now, more than ever, he can't lose his connection with God. However, I fear he will only do the opposite.

So, that brings me here to Monica. I know by doing this I'm setting things in motion. They have a lot in common and I know together, they can have peace, have what was ripped from my fingers. Normally, I would be angry at the thought but this place, it's doing something to me, something good.

I know what I need to do.

For Monica.

For Sam.

And for myself.

If there was anyone I would want Sam to start over with, it would be Monica. She's kind, understanding, God-fearing, and I know they could be happy together. She would help him run the restaurant and they would find stability in one another. I couldn't want anything more for them both.

I smile as Monica bends forward, running her thin fingers through her dark brown hair, forming it together to place a hair tie at the base of her neck. She straightens up as one of the new male barkeeps walks up to start a conversation with her about stock, from the sound of things. She walks him through his question without breaking a sweat.

She knows this restaurant better than Sam might.

I laugh.

The man walks away.

Now's my chance.

I close my eyes and reach out with my mind, searching, feeling, knocking on the barrier around her mind, hoping, praying she will let me in. I feel it start to budge, and move and then it flies open. I'm surrounded by images of Monica and her family, Monica at the restaurant and...and Sam. I can see him through her eyes, and she sees him as I do; handsome, tall, smart, funny, kind, and a man that any woman would be lucky to have. For the first time, I have no doubt I'm doing the right thing.

Before I can focus, I'm pulled to another thought, another image of Monica and me. I can feel her pain, her loss as it pulls in something deeper, something darker. My loss has only reminded her of the absence of her sister. I feel a strong tug on my heart, and I know now that Sam doesn't only need Monica, but she needs him too.

I push further, deeper until I reach...nothing.

A blank page.

And I know I have reached my destination. I place my thoughts, my hopes, my understanding in this place, in Monica's mind. Hoping she will understand, hoping she will follow the crumbs I am leaving.

"Monica, you alright?" I hear a male's voice coming to my ears. No, to Monica's.

"I." I can sense her uncertainty. "I'm fine, Robert. Thank you."

"Are you sure?"

Uneasiness spreads through her every nerve and I can feel it as my own as the hair rises on my arms. I try to focus; I still have more work.

"I'm..."

I feel a hand on my elbow, no Monica's elbow. It's becoming hard to tell the difference.

"You look pale."

Monica raises her hand to her now moisture-covered forehead. "I'm...I'm feeling a little lightheaded."

"Here, come sit down."

I feel him usher her over to the benches nearby.

She sits.

I don't stop.

"What's wrong?"

"I'm not sure."

"Should I call Sam?"

Her heart stops.

"No."

"Are you sure? I think you could use a break and well, we need one of you here to run the restaurant."

She whispers. "I know."

"So, let me call him."

I feel the numbness spreading through her body.

"No, he needs to be where he is."

Confusion vibrates in his tone. "I don't understand. We haven't seen or heard from him in days. That's not like him."

"He's going through something. Trust me we need to let him be. I planned on going to see him tomorrow after work."

Unsure, he asks, "Is there anything we can do?"

"Sadly, I don't think there is anything anyone can do for Sam. This is something he needs to go through on his own."

"Alright, then, but I do think you need to take a few days off."

"I can't. Like you said, one of us needs to be here."

He sighs in defeat. "OK, then. At least sit here for a little while longer. Try to get your head right."

"Will do."

The man starts to walk away but stops at the kitchen door. "And Monica."

"Yes, Robert."

"Please, remember you need to take care of yourself, too."

She nods as she forces a smile on her face.

Once the man disappears behind the door, Monica sighs in exhaustion as she leans forward to place her face in her hands.

Done.

I pull back, letting the door close behind me. In moments, I am looking at Monica, happy to no longer be inside her head. I see Robert exit the kitchen doors with a glass of liquid in his right hand. He walks over to where Monica is still sitting and offers it to her.

"Drink this."

She smiles shyly. "Thank you, but you didn't need to-"

He cuts her off. "I know I didn't need to, I wanted to. If you forget to take care of yourself, one of us has to." He smiles.

She takes the glass from his outstretched hand and places it on her dry lips. She quickly ingests the contents of the glass, and I can see a new energy coming over her as she closes her eyes and releases a sigh.

"Thank you, again."

"You're welcome. Take ten more minutes."

She opens her eyes, and I can see a new shine in them. "No, I'm good, that was just what I needed."

"Are you sure?"

She stands up abruptly. "Yup, I'm as tough as nails once more."

Robert chuckles as he shakes his head. "Whatever you say. You're in charge."

She hands him back the glass and shoots him a goofy look as she says. "And don't you forget it."

Another laugh rumbles through his chest. "I won't."

Monica walks away as a genuine smile takes place on her face and I can hear her say one name in her thoughts which makes me smile in return.

Sam.

Newfound Respect

Sam

I can hear my parents talking from the other room, no matter how low they try to keep their voices. After my mother ended our conversation, she got up and walked out of the room, leaving my father to follow. I didn't move. How could I? I've never heard my mother sound so defeated. I can see she's scared for me, and I don't want her to be, but at the same time, I can't change how I feel and what's clawing away inside of me.

I know I shouldn't, but I get up and make my way over to the wall and hide behind it, trying to hear them better. I feel like a little kid again, eavesdropping on my parent's private conversations.

"I'm afraid for him, Joshua."

"As am I." My father sounds exhausted.

"What are we going to do? He's so angry, so lost. If he doesn't open up, doesn't turn to our Lord for help, I'm afraid to see what he will become without Him and without Jane to lead him back to Him."

"The darkness, the devil, is an evil thing. Once it has its claws in you, it doesn't let its hold go so easily."

My mother sighs before saying in a whisper, "I know. I know."

"If anyone can reach him, it's you, my dear." The confidence in her is clear in his words.

"I'm afraid that time has long gone."

"Why do you say that?"

"He's no longer our little boy, he is a man."

"Yes, but you are his mother and that bond you have always had, it's still there."

I peer around the corner to see them looking out the back window, my father's hand on my mother's back, trying to comfort her.

"It was."

My father looks at her with confusion.

"I feel this version of our son won't be reached, not by me."

"We have to have faith."

"I'm trying to, my love, but I fear that this loss has taken something from him and replaced that good with nothing but anger."

"Then we must help him be rid of it."

"I don't know how we can. He must want the help and I can see in his eyes he doesn't. Not yet."

"But he will, and when he does, we will be here."

She places her hand on my father's cheek as she smiles at him lovingly. "Why has it always been so hard for you to show your love to him as you have shown me?"

He looks as shocked as I feel at her words. "I."

"You are not your father, Joshua. You must remember that."

"A boy cannot become a man if his father coddles him."

She scoffs. "How would you know? Maybe that's just what he needed."

"He had you. That was always more than enough."

She lowers her hand till it rests over his heart. "You don't believe that. I know you have craved a stronger bond with him, yet you always pulled back and I never understood why, and I don't care to. However, if there was ever a time to change that, now would be it."

"If he won't listen to you, he sure as heck isn't going to listen to me."

She smiles at him softly. "You never know. He might surprise you."

"What do you want me to do?"

She places her hand in his. "Just talk to him. His anger is swallowing him whole. Remind him of what the grace of God can do. What peace God can bring if he only lets Him."

"For you, I will try." He says as he raises their joined hands to his lips and lightly places a kiss on the back of hers.

I feel my heart retract.

These are the moments I will miss the most. Moments I lost out with Jane, to one day be talking about our child, to have been able to grow old with each other. How am I supposed to let this go? How am I supposed to move past this, forget her, and move on with my life when she was meant to be my future?

"Sam."

So lost in my thoughts I hadn't noticed my parents re-enter the room. I look up to see them both staring at me in concern.

"Sorry, I was…I was going to get something to drink and then…then I started thinking and got lost in my thoughts."

"That can be an easy thing to do. One must remember how to escape them." My father says.

"Yes."

My mother smiles as she takes me by the hand. "Well, it seems you have done that."

I smile at her lovingly. "Thanks to you."

I bend down and take her in my arms. I can feel her surprise as her body stays rigid for a moment longer than normal. Then her body becomes loose like cooked spaghetti as she hugs me back.

"Oh, my poor boy."

I fight back the tears. "I don't know what to do. I don't know how to make it back from this."

My father places his hand on my shoulder as I still hug my mother. "Don't worry. We will be here to help you every step of the way." I see the light drain from his eyes. "But I won't lie, son. It's not going to be an easy ride and it's going to take time. You're going to hurt." He pauses, wanting to say the right words I suppose, "You're going to be angry, and you are going to want to get lost in the darkness and the way it feels because it will lie to you. It will make you forget; make you feel good, but don't let it win. Remember, there is nothing but lies and an endless, hopeless, loveless life in the dark." His eyes are searching mine now. "You must remember the light, the warmth, the love, the hope, and joy that was once there and can be there again. Don't let the darkness win, son." He pauses, unsure of his next words. "It's not what Jane would have wanted."

* * *

My parents spent the night. I offered my room since it was too hard to sleep in there again, but they decided to sleep in the living room with me. I told them it was unnecessary, but they insisted, and I was too tired to argue. They left early the next morning, wanted to head home take care of a few things, and pack a couple of bags. I told them they did not need to come back and stay with me, but they insisted and again, I was too tired to argue and a part of me was happy for their company. I told them Monica would be stopping over today to check in, so they didn't need to return till tomorrow. I could tell my mother didn't like the idea, but my father helped her see my way.

Having them here, it helped. It didn't take away the anger completely, but I can feel it lessening, which is better than nothing, right? I look at the clock to see it read 6:28 p.m. and I find myself wondering where the time went. I know Monica will be here shortly as the restaurant closes at 7 pm. So, I decided to make myself something to eat while I wait and maybe read a book or something.

* * *

My stomach bubbles, letting me know I am happy with my choice of dinner, no matter how much I'm kicking myself in the butt for it. I mean, I'm a chef at the best restaurant in town and I make lousy mac and cheese for dinner. Who does that? I guess I should just be happy that I made something and got it down at this point. Progress is progress after all, right?

I sigh.

I glance over to see the clock reads 8:43 pm and I'm surprised that I can't tell whether I feel happy or disappointed that Monica hasn't shown up yet. Part of me still wants to be alone, craves it almost, but the rest of me knows that I shouldn't be. More than that, I know it's not what Jane would want for me and I for her if the shoes were reversed.

I would be lying if I said a part of me still hasn't owned that this is my new normal, that I'm even awake for that matter. I still can't believe she's gone. The thought alone cripples me. The thought of her takes the air from my lungs and threatens to bring me to my knees. I can feel something more than anger lingering in the depths of my soul. I know what it is, what threatens to take hold. Something more terrifying than anger. Anger can pass, come and go, but this is harder to fight back, harder to escape once it digs its teeth into you.

Depression.

I never thought of myself as someone who could get depressed. I have seen others around me suffer and struggle with it and always found myself wishing there was something I could do to help, but I knew there wasn't anything to be done. Depression isn't something that you let happen, it just does and once it does, it takes over every part of you.

There is no escape.

People say you can fight it, be better, don't let it control you. However, I've seen people fight to be free of it, to find something, anything in their lives to bring them joy again. However, nine times out of ten, they have no luck in the endeavor. I would be lying if I said the thought didn't terrify me.

I never looked wrongly at anyone who suffered from it. If anything, I wanted to understand it. But that didn't mean I wanted to join the club. Way to sound snotty.

I release another suppressed sigh, closing my eyes as the air escapes between my lips. Walking around this cool, quiet house only lets these thoughts, these feelings creep into me that much more. I want to be alone, I want to not think about anything that took place a few days ago. I want to be woken up and be able to believe this is only a dream, but I know deep down it's not what I need. I need people, anyone, to be here, even if it's only to sit with me. I need someone to get me out of my head and feelings.

I need Jane.

I open my eyes hesitantly and head for the living room couch knowing I will not be going upstairs, not anytime soon at least. I find myself longing for sleep if only to wake up to my parents here once more.

I never thought I would be begging for my father to be here, but I am.

I'm losing this fight. If it's not the anger taking hold, it's the depression rushing up to meet me in the eyes. I know if I let it in it will consume me, take me over. It's not something I want to let happen. I don't want to be this person, someone that I know Jane wouldn't be proud of. But more than that, I don't want to be one of those people I couldn't help. If I couldn't help them, how is anyone going to help me, even when I find myself ready for it?

Knock. Knock.

I look over my shoulder to stare at the door in confusion for one second too long. My eyes open wide as I jump from the couch and make my way over to the door and swing it open.

"I'm sorry, Monica, I almost forgot you said you were coming by tonight."

She smiles at me shyly. "No, I should apologize. I'm sure you thought I forgot. I finished at the restaurant a little later than I would have liked."

"Everything alright?"

She waves off my concern. "Yes. Nothing for you to worry about. I just wanted to make sure everything was closed down properly and ready for the morning."

"Thank you, Monica."

"No need to thank me."

"Yes, I do. If it weren't for you the restaurant would have lost a lot of money and customers these last few days."

70

She looks to the ground as her cheeks flush crimson. "I don't mind. I told you not to worry about anything and I meant it." She glances back up at me. "I wish I could do more, but I'm happy I can at least put your mind at ease on this if nothing else."

I'm about to say something else, but then I realize I haven't invited her in, and my face turns to one of annoyance. I can see in her eyes that she thinks it's because of her, so I smile to reassure her.

"I'm sorry. How rude of me. Please, come in. I wasn't thinking."

She looks down at her feet once more as she walks through the threshold.

"Would you like anything to drink or eat? I made…. I made mac and cheese." I laugh.

She glances over her shoulder at me. "I'm fine, thank you."

I gesture to the couch. "Please, have a seat."

"You are being weird tonight, Sam."

I rub the hair on the back of my neck as I chuckle. "Am I?"

She looks at me concerned.

"I…"

"How are you doing?"

"I'm fine."

Monica smiles at me softly. "You don't need to act fine around me, Sam. If anyone can understand, it is me."

"I know. I'm just…I'm not sure what I am right now, honestly."

"I understand."

"I feel like I'm still in a dream."

"It's going to be some time before that changes, I'm afraid."

"I wish I could just jump over it. Go a year, five years into the future."

"It wouldn't change anything."

I look at her sadly, still standing behind the couch. Is this really what my life and future have become? Years of thinking about and missing her? Wondering what our lives would have been like? Being angry with God and myself?

"Sam."

"Huh?"

"Please, come sit."

I smile, suppressing another laugh. I don't know why it was so hard for me to relax when someone was here, but when no one was here, all I did was sit on this couch. Nothing feels right. I'm different. Everything about me, about this house, is different.

"Sam."

"Sorry."

She places her hand on mine gently. "You don't need to apologize. I was only asking how your day was."

"Oh, um, my parents stopped by."

I can read the excitement in her eyes. "That's great."

"Yeah."

"How did it go? I'm getting the sense something happened."

I smile at her sheepishly. "I don't know if I ever mentioned my father to you before."

She shakes her head indicating I haven't.

"Well, we've never really gotten along."

"Oh, please don't tell me you had a fight."

"Kind of."

"Do they know about…"

She stops not wanting to bring Jane up.

"Yes. Someone told them."

Monica looks worried as she says, "And he still fought with you?"

I feel my eyebrows meeting in the middle of my face. "It wasn't like that."

I can see the confusion forming on her face.

"I kind of said something I shouldn't have."

"Like?"

I shift uneasily. "I said I was angry with God."

"Well, I think right now you're entitled to feel that way."

"I agree. However, my parents, especially my father, are deeply religious."

"As am I."

"I know."

She cuts me off. "It will pass, Sam. I've been where you are. I've felt that same anger and it took me some time to find my way back to him."

"It's hard for me to think about. I've never missed mass. Never missed a day of prayer. Jane and I were so close because of our faith and for me to feel this way, so disconnected from Him, makes me feel disconnected from her."

"I understand."

Looking in her eyes, I'm unsure. "Do you?"

She nods. "My sister was the religious one. I believed and prayed here and there, but I wasn't really what you might call religious. After her death, I was so angry at God. She was so devoted to Him, and He let that happen to her."

"How did that change your faith?"

Her smile sends a comforting warmth over me. "It took a long time, but after I truly grieved, I thought about her. I thought about how much she loved God and prayed, and I knew the life I was living, the anger inside of me isn't what she would have wanted for me. I also knew I had never felt so distant from her. In that moment I realized letting go of the anger, giving it to God, and truly letting Him in would only make me closer to her. Letting Him comfort and mend me, letting Him fill my soul and life with joy and prayer would only make her happy. So, I did just that."

I look at her with pain-filled eyes. "Did that help?"

"Honestly, yes. It took some time and a lot of work on my end, but it did help. I felt closer to her, and I started to find peace again."

I look out the window. "I want that more than anything. I want to go back to what life was before all of this."

"Life will never be exactly as it was."

I close my eyes. "I know." I open them, "But I can tell myself it will be."

She smiles at me sadly. "Have you tried talking to her?"

"To whom?"

She hesitates for a moment. "To Jane."

I feel my eyebrows meet in the middle of my face. "You mean her spirit?"

She nods.

I turn away. "No, I haven't."

"It might help."

"I don't know how. It's not like she can talk back."

She glances down at her interlocked fingers. "No, but it may give you some peace."

"What would I even say?"

"Tell her the truth. Tell her you miss her, you are angry and feel alone, that you don't know what to do now that she's gone. Ask her for help, for guidance."

"I don't know."

She places a hand on mine lightly. "I know it seems crazy, but I promise it will help."

I look down at our hands as warmth spreads through them and up my arm and I feel lighter. She smiles at me before she removes her from mine.

"So, how about I make us a snack and we hang out and watch a few movies until you're ready to call it a night?"

"You don't mind?"

"No, the restaurant is closer to here anyway."

She pauses and her face turns to one of embarrassment, almost as if she just realized what she said.

"I didn't mean to."

I cut her off with a smile. "No, I would like it if you stayed. The quiet only makes my mind darker. If you would like to stay, I would like that. You can take our room or the spare room. I've been sleeping on the couch."

I can see in her eyes she wants to say something.

"Sam."

"Yes?"

She turns away from me as she releases a sigh, "I have to tell you something."

I shift nervously in my seat. "What is it?"

"It was me." She says without looking in my direction.

"What was you?"

She hesitates for a moment before lifting her head to have her eyes meet mine. "I called your parents. I didn't want you to be alone in this."

Baffled, I froze.

"I'm sorry. I didn't mean to overstep. I thought I was doing the right thing. I remember how I was when I lost my sister and I know having people around is important right now."

I force a light smile as I look in the direction of the kitchen. "It's fine. I understand."

She frees a long sigh from between her parted lips. "Oh, thank God."

"But, how did you have their number to call in the first place?"

"The restaurant's files. You have one in there too, remember?"

She gets up and makes her way to my kitchen, leaving me to sit alone on the couch once more.

"Pick out a few movie options."

I yell over my shoulder. "Sure."

I walk over to our movie shelf, hundreds of movies to pick from. I run my hands along them in a numb zombie fashion. For a moment I find myself wondering what Jane would think about Monica spending the night. She's only here to keep me company, keep me sane. Wouldn't I want the same for her if roles were reversed? Yes. I know I would. Everyone can use a friend, especially at a time like this.

STAGE FOUR:

Depression

Sam

After Monica left, I was alone once more, and my parents couldn't get here fast enough. Alone, the silence creeps in and I find myself in the darkness fighting to keep my head above water.

I can feel the depression fighting harder to take hold of me. The anger gets cast away, only to be replaced by something more sinister, something darker, harder, and not as easy to fight or let go of. Depression is a darkness of the mind, but it's not what people think or believe it to be. It's not something that doesn't exist because you can't physically see it and it's not something that someone can just medicate themselves to fix. Most of all, it's not something you can get over or push off to the side. No matter how badly you find yourself wanting to, no matter how much you wish to escape it, clawing your way out isn't possible. Once it has you, you are there until it decides it will let you breathe once more.

I know I am at my last resort and I'm losing this fight. I think about what Monica said last night as I sigh and close my eyes to say one word, one name.

"Jane."

This is crazy.

"I don't know if you can hear me or if you are even here, but I miss you. I'm so lost."

* * *

Jane

I watch Sam as he sits alone in the house once more. I want to find a way to reach him, but I don't know how. I thought getting Monica to go there and talk with him, to keep him company, would have helped more than it had. They had some great conversations, so great that I saw the anger leaving Sam's body long before it finally did. I thought it helped, but now, looking at him, I'm not so sure. It's like something else, something darker, is taking hold.

"Jane."

My jaw drops in surprise.

"I don't know if you can hear me or if you are here, but I miss you. I'm so lost."

"I miss you too," I say in a whisper, knowing it doesn't matter either way. He can't hear me.

Pain pushes behind my eyes as tears begin to form. Seeing him like this, almost a week later, it's hard. I know that a week isn't much time, but I hate seeing him like this. I know I can't do much from where I am, but there has to be something.

"I'm fighting so hard to keep the anger away, to find my way back to the man I was before this all happened. But I'm afraid to admit I think I'm losing that battle. The anger is less now, but I feel something worse taking over. I don't care to move off the couch, to eat, bathe. I find myself not wanting to do anything but sit and sleep. I'm a shell of the man you knew, the man you loved since you left. I'm fighting so hard to get him back, but I'm losing. I get over one hurdle only to find something bigger in its wake."

I focus as hard as I can, willing him to hear me. "No, you're not, Sam. You are the strongest person I know. You can make it through this, and you will. You will have happy days again. Like Monica and your parents told you, it takes time."

He looks up with a touch of a smile on his face. "You were my best friend. The person I would come to, to help me get through something like this. Now I don't know who to turn to. My parents are trying, and Monica has been great, but it's not the same." He pauses and looks up to where I am standing, in my room, here in...in heaven. "No one can be you."

Knock. Knock.

I turn to look at my door but realize it was Sam's.

* * *

Sam

I wipe away the tears with the back of my arm as I make my way to the front door. I pull it open slowly.

"We're back." My father says in a tone that he's trying to keep light, for my benefit, I'm sure.

"How are you feeling today Sam?" My mother says from his side.

"Better." I lie.

She's not buying it.

"Can we come in?" She asks in a soft tone.

"Of course."

She brushes my arm with her hand on the way past.

"Did your friend Monica ever stop by?" She asks as I close the door behind them.

"Yes."

"Good. I'm glad you had some company."

"Me too."

Silence fills the air between us.

My father breaks it awkwardly. "Were you able to track down the paperwork we talked about?"

My mother's gaze falls upon him.

"No. Haven't had much time to look."

Ignoring my mother's glare, he continues. "Maybe that's where we should start."

"Joshua, I think we can wait a little bit."

I cut her off. "No, he's right. I would rather get it done now."

* * *

Sam

With the three of us, it took little time to locate. My father is the one who found them in the back of Jane's nightstand. When he announced to us he had located them, my mother went to his side and plucked them from his hand saying, "I'll take those."

Something that looked a lot like shock took over my father's expression. "Silvia."

"Not another word. We found them. Now, let's take some time to relax and settle in. We are going to be here for some time."

I look at my father. "She's right."

"Of course, she is. I've never known your mother to be wrong."

We all laugh a little at the comment, knowing how true it was.

She glances at my father as she says in a low voice, "We can look these over later tonight."

He nods in agreement.

"For now, let's talk about what we can make for lunch."

I smile at her. Forgetting how nice it was to have her so close by.

* * *

My parents did exactly as my mother said they would. She didn't want me to have to worry about anything to do with the preparations for Jane's funeral and I haven't. She and my father looked over all the papers and made all the calls needed in the following days after they arrived. Everything was set. Jane's funeral is in a few hours.

I will be saying goodbye to my wife, my best friend and it will be final. I'm having a hard time figuring out how I am supposed to say goodbye to someone who's been my whole life for so long; someone I woke up to every morning and went to sleep next to every night. How do you say goodbye to someone who was there every day for years of your life and who became your shoulder, your world, your everything? How am I going to say goodbye to her?

"Sam?"

My mother's soft voice comes from my bedroom doorway to me sitting on the king-size bed.

"Hey, Mom, is everything alright?"

She takes a step inside the room, "I was about to ask you the same thing."

I peer at the picture of Jane and me on our honeymoon that is sitting on my nightstand. "I was just thinking."

"About the funeral?"

I nod.

"I know it's going to be a hard day but once we get through it, things will be a little easier. I promise."

"What if I don't want them to be easier?"

I can hear the confusion in her tone. When I turn back to look at her it's plain on her face. "What do you mean?"

"I don't want to forget her."

She smiles at me softly as she closes the distance between us and sits on the bed next to me. "No one said to forget her, honey."

"Goodbye always ends in forget."

She places her hand lightly on mine. "Not if you don't let it."

"It's hard to explain."

"I understand more than you think."

I smile at her. "I have no doubt, Momma. It's all still so confusing to me though. It hurts so much to think about her, but the thought of forgetting her, of leaving her in my past, that hurts so much more."

"Because she meant so much to you and she should. When someone comes into our lives it is always for a reason. Some we encounter for a moment of time and others stay with us much longer. Everyone serves a purpose and with Jane, she became a huge part of your life, your world and your heart. Because of that, she deserves to stay there and not be forgotten."

"But how do I honor her, hold onto her, and heal at the same time?"

She lightly pats my hand. "That is something you need to figure out for yourself I'm afraid."

I close my eyes and exhale.

"It will get better. I know right now you're still having a hard time with the simplest of things, but in more time, you'll do things without thinking, like you once did."

"I hate feeling like this."

"I know, my love."

"I feel like I'm dishonoring her by being this version of myself."

"Then honor her and fight harder to be the man you were before this tragedy, the man she loved more than anything in this world. Be the person she would still want you to be."

I open my eyes and turn to her. "I'm trying."

"I know you are, and I know she knows too."

"I hope so. The last few days I've come a long way. I'm still angry, sad, and lost but I'm trying not to be angry with God. I'm working on getting my faith back and remembering that God didn't do this, no one did. It was her time, as hard and as messed up as it all is."

"Just keep doing what you're doing. Take one day at a time, one more step forward."

She's right and I know how lucky I am to have her here with me now. Helping, guiding and reminding me of things I would otherwise forget in this time. She has always been there, always known how to reach me and I thank God that He made her my mom.

"Thanks, Mom, for everything."

"You don't need to thank me, it's what a mother is here for."

"But some mothers aren't and more times than not you go beyond most mothers I know and for that, I want to thank you; for always being there and never giving up on me. I'm blessed to have you as my mother, and I wanted you to know that."

"Oh, my precious boy." She holds back tears as she kisses me on the cheek. "I think it's time for dinner and then we should head over to the church for the vigil."

I nod as she pulls me along out the door.

The Funeral

Sam

As the priest searched the pews with his eyes, I could see the sadness in them. Father Emerson had been our priest since we came to live here. He hadn't known me very long; however, he knew Jane almost her whole life and I could see the pain on his face at the loss of her.

She would stop by a couple of times a month to see if they needed any help running the soup kitchen or gathering food or clothing for those in need. Jane always thought of everyone, one of the many reasons I came to love her so much. It was because of her that I was as involved with our church as I was.

Father Emerson rests his sorrow-filled eyes on me before he starts to speak. "Receive the Lord's blessing. The Lord bless you and watch over you. The Lord make His face shine upon you and be gracious to you. The Lord look kindly on you and give you peace. In the Name of the Father, and of the Son and of the Holy Spirit."

In unison, we all reply, "Amen."

Father Emerson was more Jane's priest than mine. He has been the one to give her all her sacraments growing up. I still remember the day she brought me to this church for the first time and introduced us. I had known many priests throughout my life, being brought up catholic myself, but Father Emerson was someone I truly respected. He was a priest in every sense of the word and the kindest soul I had ever met.

"Sam."

I turn to see my mother and father standing next to me.

"It's time to go up and say goodbye."

I look ahead once more to the casket up at the altar, the casket that holds my wife. For a moment I'm frozen again. I know I must stand, move but I'm finding it hard. I hear my father whisper something to my mother, but I'm lost in this moment. I feel a firm hand on my shoulder as it applies a little pressure pulling me from my mind. I look up to see my father looking down at me with a smile that holds much sadness.

"Come on, son. I'll help you."

He moves his hand under my arm swiftly, before anyone else could notice, and pulls me up from my wooden pew with an easy grace.

Without looking at him I whisper, "Thanks, Dad."

Without a word we proceed into the aisle as I take one heavy step at a time, slowly moving forward.

"Take your time." My father whispers behind me, his hand still helping me along.

Just five more steps and you are there.

You can do this.

You need to do this.

Suddenly, calm washes over me and I don't feel my father's hand on me anymore, instead, I feel. I feel.

Jane.

I look all around me frantically.

"Sam." My father whispers. "Sam. Are you alright?"

I feel her. I know she's here. She's standing here, with me, helping me get through this moment as she has with everything else in life. I smile sadly.

"I'm ok, Dad." I place a hand on his letting him know I can make it the rest of the way on my own.

He looks at me unsure, but after a moment nods at me proudly and releases his grip on me. I take the last few steps towards my wife's body with a new eagerness. I place my hands on the side of the coffin and look down at her for the last time. I bend over and kiss her ice-cold forehead.

As I pull back, I whisper. "I know you are here with me. Thank you for not leaving my side. I don't know what I'm going to do now without you, but I pray you will be here along the way helping me, and guiding me. You were always my angel. You found me in the darkest time of my life and showed me the light was still there for me to embrace and now...now you are my angel in every sense of the word. Please, don't leave my side, not yet. I still need you. I need you to show me that light still exists. I need you to lead me there one last time, my love."

I stand up straight feeling the anger, the darkness leaving me slowly as I turn away and head down the aisle to the open door and out into the cool air. As it hits me in the face, I feel a new energy and lightness wash over me. And for the first time during all of this, I know everything is going to be OK.

"Just take one day at a time," I say to myself as I look to the heavens. "Just one day."

* * *

Jane

I place my hand on his shoulder hoping to comfort him. I close my eyes and send out all my energy to my fingertips willing them to stay on his shoulder and to let him feel my presence. I know he does once his whispers reach my ears and I feel a smile form on my face. All I've wanted to do was make this easier for him. To let him know I'm always going to be here if he needs me and that I'm ok. I want him to know that I want him to find peace again and to not stop living his life.

I try to push all these thoughts onto him through my hand. I need him to know things aren't always going to be like this, that he will find happiness again, and that I want that for him. Death is easy, it's being left behind and living without the one you lost that's hard. I have it easy which leaves me only to imagine how painful this has been for him.

I couldn't imagine what I would do if the roles were reversed. I hope that I would know he was at peace and that he would want me to keep living my life. I would like to think that I would be able to let go and feel at peace with his loss, but the truth is I don't know. I know that like me, he would want me to be happy and continue living but in the moment of his loss, I don't know if that would be something that would register for me.

All I can do is try to let him know in my thoughts and through my touch how I feel and what I want for him.

"Just take one day at a time," Sam says to himself as he looks to the heavens. "Just one day."

"That's right, Sam. One day at a time."

I smile at him lovingly as I feel my energy being stripped from my body and I know I don't have much time left. I focus my energy once more and give his shoulder a light squeeze before I release him.

"I love you, Sam. Things are going to get better. I promise."

* * *

Sam

I watch in a zombie-like fashion as they throw the last shovel of dirt on a newly marked grave, Jane's grave; the last step of goodbye. I make a promise to myself to come here at least once a week to see her, talk with her, in hopes that in some way I'll never truly lose her.

"Sam."

I turn to see Monica only a few steps away now.

"Hey. Thanks for coming."

"Of course, don't be silly. I loved Jane."

I turn back to the fresh dirt at my feet. "You would have been crazy not to."

"She was so easy to get along with, no one could say otherwise."

"It was a nice turnout, don't you think?"

I can hear the smile in her voice. "Did you expect any less?"

I smile weakly, "No, it was everything I hoped. Nothing short of what she deserved."

"So many people had such wonderful things to say about her, such beautiful stories and memories. It was a beautiful service, Sam."

I nod.

"I'll wait for you in the parking lot."

I turn around to look at her once more. "You don't have to do that."

"I know I don't have to. I want to."

She turns to walk away but not before saying, "Take your time, Sam. No rush, OK?"

I nod once more as she turns away and I focus my attention once more on the place where my Jane now rests, a place that I will now visit once a week and a place that will always hold a piece of my heart.

It's a weird feeling, not feeling whole. My heart still beats the same, yet it's different. A piece will always remain here with her, and I wouldn't have it any other way. If it hadn't been for Jane, I don't know where my life would have ended up. She got me back on my path and helped me lead the life I always wanted. Because of her, I took the chance on the restaurant, which is booming. I bought a house and became the best version of myself. I owe so much to her, more than I ever told or thanked her for.

I know without a doubt that God sent her to me right now when I needed her light the most. Everyone has been saying we meet everyone for a reason, and I don't doubt that now. She played the most important part of all. She was my angel, my guide back to the light. Without her, my life would have been meaningless and I know it's a life she would want me to keep living.

Now I know the best way to honor her and keep her in my heart is to live. She would want me to find peace and start my life over, to do everything we talked about. I plan on it, but I also know it's going to take me some time.

Baby steps.

But I'll get there.

"I'll be that person again, the man you fell in love with. Just give me some time and help me. Lead me to the light once more. You will always be in my heart, Jane. There won't be a day I don't think about you. No matter where my life ends up, you will always be there with me. I will never forget you and I will always be grateful for what you did and continue to do for me. Thank you for choosing me and for being my angel. I love you. Always and forever."

I close my eyes and take in a deep slow breath before opening them once more.

"This isn't goodbye. It's until we meet again."

I bend over and place my hand on the mound of dirt reaching out my thoughts and words hoping, praying she can hear me.

"Until we meet again. Be at peace my love and I will try to do the same."

Baby Steps

One month later

Sam

Entering the restaurant for the first time in over a month sends shock waves through my body. I know it's time to return to what my life was before...before my loss, but it doesn't make it any easier. If it wasn't for my parents and Monica, I don't know where I would be right now. I also made a promise to Jane that I intend to keep.

"Sam!"

I turn to see Robert walking in my direction with a smile.

"Wow, it's great to see you, man. We've missed you around here." He looks around frantically and lowers his voice. "Not that Monica hasn't been great but it's nice to have the man back if you know what I mean."

A genuine smile creeps up on my face as I slap him on the shoulder in a greeting. I lean in and whisper, "I know what you mean."

Robert's body vibrates from the chuckle that escapes his body and I can't help but laugh in unison with him.

"How have you been, man? I wanted to stop by but wanted to give you some time, and didn't want to intrude."

"You could never do that. But I appreciate the thought and the space. I'm handling things better but still have a long way to go."

I can see the sadness as it creeps into his eyes. "That's to be expected."

I whisper, "So everyone keeps telling me."

"What?"

I smile at him sheepishly. "Nothing. So how is the restaurant doing?"

"Still amazing. We have been booked out almost every day since the last time you were in."

I turned to him in surprise. "For dinner?"

"For lunch and dinner."

"Wow. Really?" I rub at the hair on the back of my head.

"It's been crazy busy, and money has been flowing in. Monica also found a cheaper vendor to get the food from."

"Really?"

Robert laughs. "Yes. She's been amazing. Been running the place almost better than you." He smiles playfully. "Almost."

I grin. "No one does it better than me."

"You can say that again, boss. It is great to see you."

"Thanks, Robert. By the way, how is the family doing?"

I can see the hesitation in his eyes. The uncertainty on how to answer the question is clear as he stumbles over his words. "Everyone is doing great."

"Robert, you can be more specific. I appreciate you trying to watch my feelings, but I wouldn't have asked if I didn't want to know. So, I'll ask again, how are Rebecca and the kids doing?"

I see the reluctance in his eyes disappear as it's replaced with admiration. Not sure if it's for me or his family when he answers. "Joe and Mary are doing great. Getting so big. Hard to believe Mary will be going into sixth grade this year and Joe into fourth. Rebecca is doing well, we are...we are expecting."

"She's pregnant?"

He nods.

I throw my arm around his shoulder and give him a light squeeze. "You dog. Man, another one, huh?"

He smiles. "Yea. We are pretty excited."

"As you should be. Do you know yet what it will be?"

He shakes his head no. "Still another month before we can find out the sex. Still pretty early."

"As long as mother and child are healthy, I'm sure you'll both be happy."

He nods. "Thanks, Sam."

"No thanks needed. So, where's Monica?"

"In the kitchen doing inventory, I believe."

I remove my arm from around his neck and tap him on the shoulder. "Thanks."

I start to walk away as Robert calls out.

"Sam."

"Yeah?"

"She's pretty amazing."

Confused, I asked. "Who?"

"Monica. Just thought you should know." He says with a smile before turning away.

* * *

Sam

"Hey, you."

Monica turns slowly towards me. Once her eyes come to rest on my face, a smile forms on hers and I can't help but mimic it in return.

She puts the towels in her hands on the counter and walks over to me.

"Hey, yourself. I didn't know you were coming in today."

I shrug. "I figured it was time."

Her smile lessons slightly. "Only if you're ready. There's no reason to rush." Her smile becomes whole once more. "I have everything under control, after all."

I chuckle as I look around at the kitchen, cleaner and more organized than I remember.

"I can see that."

Her slap to my shoulder brings my attention back to her.

"But really how are you doing today?"

"I'm fine."

She looks at me unsure.

"Really. I just wish everyone would stop asking me how I am and looking at me like I'm a puppy who gets beat every day."

Her smile disappears completely. "I'm sorry, Sam. I didn't mean...I just want to make sure you're doing alright."

She starts to walk back over to the counter, but I stop her by grabbing her wrist lightly.

"I know you do, and it means a lot. I didn't mean to make you feel like you were doing something wrong. I know you are trying to help. You and my parents have been a blessing in this. I don't want you to think I'm not grateful, because I am. Without the three of you, I don't know where I would be right now." I chuckle, "As I'm sure I've already told you a million times."

Her smile returns slightly, and I can see she's about to respond but I cut her off before she has the chance.

"I just...when everyone keeps asking how I am or looking at me that way, it only reminds me of what I've lost and in doing so, makes me go backward." I look her deep in the eyes. "You understand what I mean?"

She nods. "I do."

"I just want to move forward and get back to ... well, my new normal I suppose. I know it's time and I know it's what Jane would want. She wouldn't want me to stop living my life. She would want me to keep living it and have the best one I could. I know because I would want the same for her if it was me."

She places her hand lightly on my shoulder. "Then let's get you back to the living, Samuel Hawthorn."

"Oh, man, it's that bad huh?" I say with a chuckle.

She looks at me confused for a moment.

"You're using my government name so I must be in trouble." I smile.

She smiles in return. "Oh, you have no idea. You are back among the living now and I'll tell you, life in this restaurant is no picnic. It's a lot of work. Long hours, hard days and oh, man the boss."

My smile disappears, playing along with her. "That bad?"

With a nod of the head, she continues. "Oh, you're in for it. He can be a real hard ass."

"Can he now?"

She looks at me and we both erupt into an uncontrollable laughter, one that I haven't had in so long. It feels good, like the old me. I feel it from the top of my head to the end of my toes and for the first time, I don't doubt that I'm ready.

* * *

"You want to do something tonight after work?" I ask the question to Monica's back.

The restaurant closes in a few hours, and it has been such a good day with her that I don't want it to end just yet. I don't want this day, this feeling, to end.

"What do you have in mind?"

"Maybe we can go for a walk along the beach and get some ice cream and just talk."

The main thing I love about living in Florida is that I am so close to the ocean. It can be so peaceful walking along it at night with no one else in sight.

Monica turns around to face me with a smile on her face as she crosses her arms over her chest. "Ice cream?"

My smile disappears. "Ye-es. I thought you liked ice cream?"

Her arms fall to her sides as a laugh erupts in her chest and shakes her small body from the intensity of it.

Now it's my turn to scowl. "What's so funny?"

It takes her a second to stop laughing. She wipes away a tear and looks at me with a smile.

"I do. I'm only messing with you." She slaps a hand on my shoulder. "Lighten up already." She removes her hand from my shoulder and places it in my hand as she looks me in the eyes. "I would love to have ice cream with you, Samuel."

I look away and down to our intertwined hands and my heart stops. I must take in a deep breath before the dizziness subsides. Not wanting to hurt her, I remove my hand from hers and make my way to the kitchen door.

I look over my shoulder at her and force a smile on my face. "See you in a few hours."

I try not to notice the hurt on her face as I make my exit.

* * *

The next few hours flew by and the pit in my stomach grew bigger with each passing minute. Did Monica think I asked her out...on a date? No, she couldn't possibly have thought that, could she? No, she is just a good friend. Neither of us would ever go there. Would we? My stomach does a flop as I double over hoping I'm not about to get sick, hoping more that no one noticed. I erect myself and head for the bathroom, throw some water on my face and give myself a pep talk.

Man up. It's only a walk and some ice cream, at night, just the two of us, by the water. Oh, man. What have I done? Of course, she thought I was asking her on a date. What girl wouldn't? Everything about tonight screamed date. But why would she have said yes? I know Monica likes me enough as a boss and a friend but in that way?

More importantly, I'm not ready. Not enough time has passed for me to even think about that, to think about any woman in that way, especially not someone close to me, someone who's been there through all of it and someone who, if something went wrong, I couldn't afford to live without.

You must tell her.

What am I going to say?

My stomach flips again, and I feel the bile starting to rise as I make a run for the nearest stall. I place my arms on opposite sides resting my hands on the cool wall. Through the ringing in my ears, I hear someone else enter the restroom, and then a knock on my stall.

"Sam. Are you in there?" Robert's voice rings through the bathroom as he knocks lightly on the stall I am inhabiting.

"Yeah, I'll be out in a moment."

"Ok. Just checking. Sounded like someone was getting sick in there."

Only me.

"Also, Monica sent me to find you."

Another flop.

"Said she needs your help with something in the kitchen before we close down for the night."

"OK. Let her know I'll be right there. Thank you, Rob."

"No problem, boss."

The door clicks home, and I release a sigh I hadn't realized I'd been holding. I exit the stall and apply more water to my face. As I look in the mirror all I see is a scared, lost man.

* * *

"Rob told me you needed me."

Not turning to face me, Monica gestures with her hand over her shoulder, telling me to come closer. As I reach her side, I see our schedule book on the counter in front of her.

"Yes. I wanted to let you know we are booked out for the whole month.

People have been calling in nonstop. Ever since we added in the bar, karaoke and game night, we don't have enough tables for people who want to schedule."

"Well, that's a good thing."

"Yes."

"Isn't it?"

She sighs lightly. "It is but...a few things. Ideas, I guess I should say."

"Ok, shoot."

Still not turning to face me she continues. "For starters, we need to hire a few more people. It's too much work now with the little crew we have going, and everyone is tired."

"Done."

I can see the surprise as her shoulders shift. "Second, I think we need to consider opening the restaurant up to seven days a week and longer hours. With how many people want to book a reservation, I think it would be a smart move. At least try it out and see what happens. If we can't keep enough people in the seats, we could always change the hours back."

"Done. Anything else?"

She stays silent for a moment before turning to face me slowly. "I...yes. I think we need to think about expanding."

"Expanding?"

"Yes. Maybe start with making this restaurant bigger, then see how the rest of the year goes. If it goes well, I think we should make another restaurant about twenty or so miles from here. I think that will allow people who are too far from this location to find a nice spot closer to them. A lot of people like to have nights out, especially on the weekends. They like the idea of a place like this for a date night with karaoke or a family game night. We could do that and see how it goes. If it doesn't work, you could always sell that property after."

"I think that's a good idea."

She looks up at me for the first time. "You do?"

I smile. "Yes, I think they all are."

She nods. "Good. I'm glad."

We stand in silence for a while before I turn to walk back out into the restaurant to see if anyone else needs help.

"Sam?"

I turn around.

"I...I wanted to apologize."

"For what?"

She responds shyly. "For earlier. I...I wasn't thinking. I shouldn't have grabbed your hand like that...I."

I cross the room, put my fingers under her chin, and lift her face to look at me. "There is nothing to apologize for."

I feel her head shift as she swallows and then I realize for the first time how close we are standing to each other, bodies only eight inches apart and our faces less than five. I drop my hand and take a step back. I try to swallow, but my mouth is suddenly dry.

First time out

Sam

I look down at Monica as the wind brushes her fawn hair across her face and she tries to frantically get it under control. She looks over at me as she releases a small laugh.

"If I had known it was going to be a windy night, I would have brought something to pull my hair back."

I look at her sheepishly. "Sorry, I didn't think about that." I gesture at my lack of hair.

She releases another light laugh, "I'm glad we came out here. It's peaceful."

I nod in agreement.

"How are your parents doing?"

Her question took me by surprise, I hesitated before I answered. "They are doing good. They returned home the other day."

"Will they be making any more visits in the near future?"

I smile. "Honestly, I overheard them talking about looking for a place closer to me, so there is a good chance I'll be seeing a lot more of them."

"That's a good thing, right?"

I hesitate. "Yes and no. I would like them to be closer to see me more, but I also don't want them to worry about me so much. They have their own lives to live, you know what I mean?"

"Yes. But I also know they are your parents and being so, they will always worry about you. If living closer to you makes them do it a little less then so be it, right?"

"I guess so."

I can see her struggling with her next words like she's unsure if she should continue. "If they do move closer it would be good for you and your father, wouldn't it?"

I look at her confused. "Meaning?"

"I know you were never really close with him, but after...since everything happened, it seemed like something shifted. Am I wrong?"

I look ahead. "No."

"Sorry. I don't mean to pry."

"You're not."

We walk in silence for a few minutes before I decide where to take the conversation. "I think I'm ready to try to go back to church. It won't be easy, but I know I need to try. I'm still...angry and confused, but I need to fix my relationship with God. I know it's what I need to do, what Jane would want me to do, and I know I won't be able to fully heal until it is done."

I see a smile spread across Monica's face as she nods her head in agreement.

"I was hoping...I wanted to take someone along for moral support, I guess I should say. I was wondering if..."

I hesitate, unsure if I should continue. After what happened today at the restaurant, I'm second-guessing a lot of things.

"You wanted to know if I would go with you."

"I...if...um."

A slight giggle escapes between her lips. "I would be happy to, Sam."

"Are you sure? I don't want you to feel like you have to."

"No, I want to. I know it's a process and I would like to be there to help you through it and having been in your shoes myself, maybe I can help you with it."

I see her hand start to move towards mine. It stops at the same moment her smile disappears, almost like she realized at the last moment what she was about to do. She stares straight ahead at the horizon as I sigh.

"Monica."

"Yes."

"I wanted to talk to you about something else."

She turns her head slightly in my direction.

"About what happened earlier."

She looks away once more.

"I…"

"Sam. Really, you don't have to, it was nothing. I…it won't happen again."

"It's not that I…I'm just not there…not yet." She looks me in the eyes, and I see something in them that I've never seen before, something like hope. "I need time. I don't know if or when I'll ever be able to start over with someone new."

"I know that. I didn't-"

I cut her off. "I know you didn't, and I don't want to make this more than what it needs to be. I don't know if we could even go there, if there would ever be something there with us or not. Maybe one day. All I know is I'm not ready to think about that or explore it."

"I know, and I wouldn't ask you to do something you weren't ready for."

I stop and close my eyes. "I know."

When I open them, Monica is standing in front of me, arms around herself.

"Are you cold?"

"No, I'm fine."

I take the jacket off my shoulders and move closer to her. I wrap it around the back of her and rest it on her shoulders. It's not until it rests in place that I realize how close we are once more. I feel the pit in my stomach growing but there's something else there, too, something I've only felt once before in my life. With Jane. I close my eyes and take a step back leaving Monica to look at me in uncertainty.

"Thank you."

"Don't mention it."

I turn to start walking once more but stop as I feel her hand around my wrist.

"Sam."

I turn to face her with much hesitation.

"I want you to know I'm here. Anything you need. I don't expect or want anything in return other than your friendship if that's something you can give."

I nod.

She releases my wrist. "So, this weekend."

I look at her with confusion.

"Church."

"Oh, yeah. I would like to start as soon as possible."

"This weekend, it is."

We start walking back to the restaurant. We travel the rest of the way in an uncomfortable silence.

Last step

Jane

Watching Sam the last few weeks hasn't been easy, but now seeing how far he's come and how close he is to finding peace again makes it easier. I know it's time, the last step to get him to acceptance and hopefully to starting his new life, one without me.

I lay down in my bed and rest my hands on my chest, lost in thought.

Focusing.

Unsure, scared to do this next step but knowing it needs to be done. I know Sam and if I don't do something he will stay in this place, frozen, for years and that's something I can't let happen.

I close my eyes and concentrate.

"Monica."

Under my eyelids I see a picture forming. I wait. concentrate harder until I see her.

Monica is asleep in her bed.

I move myself closer to her sleeping body.

Focusing.

Until.

Pop. Snap.

I'm in.

Her dream is with Sam on the beach, like earlier today, but it's different. The scene in front of me is fuzzy. I strain harder to make out a clearer picture. They are holding hands, shoulders touching.

They are a couple.

I knew Monica liked Sam, but I wasn't sure how much, not until now. She has been there for him; she has been what I once was, and I know she will do anything she can to make him happy.

I know this is the right thing to do.

So why am I hesitating?

You know the answer.

I shake my head violently, keeping my eyes closed tight. There is no time for hesitation. Sam needs this, Monica needs this and...I need this.

I move closer to them on the beach and lean closer to Monica.

"Monica. I need you to listen to me."

"What?" She looks around frantically.

"Please, relax."

"Ja-Jane?"

"Yes."

"But how?" She pauses and then the realization becomes plain on her face. "I'm dreaming." She answers herself with a known fact.

"Yes, but what I'm about to say to you is not a dream."

"You're not making any sense."

"The main way people who have passed on can communicate with the living is-"

She cuts me off in shock, "Through dreams."

I nod my head forgetting for a moment she can't see me, "Yes."

She closes her eyes as she takes in a deep breath. Releases Sam's hand and turns to face where my voice is coming from. She opens her eyes slowly.

"I'm sorry."

Shocked, I ask. "For what?"

"I...I shouldn't be having a dream like this, or these kinds of thoughts."

"Monica, there is no need to apologize."

"Yes, there is. You're his wife."

"Was...was his wife. I'm gone, Monica. I can't...I can't be there for him. Not anymore. I need you to help him. I need you to be for him what I no longer can."

"What are you talking about?"

I pause but only briefly. "Do you love him?"

"I..."

"Please. I need to know."

"I...yes. Yes, I do. I'm so sorry, Jane. I never meant..."

"Please, don't. I'm happy you do."

Shock takes over her expression. "You are?"

"Yes. I couldn't ask you this otherwise."

"Whatever you need Jane."

"I want you to go to him."

Silence.

"Meaning?"

"I want you to tell him how you feel about him."

"What? No, I can't."

I squeeze my eyes closed tighter. "Yes, you can."

"Jane. It's too soon and he doesn't feel the same way. He already told me he isn't ready."

"He lied."

She shakes her head. "I can see he isn't ready."

"He doesn't want to believe he is. He doesn't want to admit or act on what he is feeling, just like you. He's afraid in doing so that he is hurting me, forgetting me." I pause finding it hard to get out the next words. "Replacing me."

"I would never-"

I cut her off. "I know you wouldn't. Which is another reason why I'm happy it's you. You can understand what he's feeling. You know it's not easy and you don't expect him to ever forget me, but you also know he has room left in his heart for someone else. For you. All you need to do is tell him."

"Tonight. I overstepped."

"No. He felt it. He wanted the same thing you did tonight. Like I said, his fears got in the way. You need to take that fear and silence it."

"Are you sure?"

"Yes. And it needs to be done now, while he's open to it. If you leave him to sit and think long enough, he will shut it out."

In the silence, I can feel her uncertainty. She cares about him and his friendship, and she's afraid to lose it, lose him.

"Jane."

"Yes."

"I'm sorry. Not for caring for him. I'm sorry your life ended so soon. I'm sorry you were taken from him and from the life you both deserved and I'm sorry that now you have to come here, to me, like this and push us towards each other."

"You would have made it there with or without me."

"Maybe one day. But you shouldn't have had to do this. I don't know if I would have been able to."

"You would have. When you love someone, you will do anything to make sure they are happy. In doing so, it brings you happiness, brings you...peace. I should go now."

"Thank you, Jane, for helping him become the man he is today and thank you for letting me help him continue to be that man."

"I will miss you both. Take care of each other."

She smiles in my direction as the dream starts to fold in on itself. I see her reach her hand out and take Sam's once more. My heart skips a beat as a chill trickles down my body and a smile forms on my face.

Stage Five:

༄༅

Acceptance

Sam

For the first time in the last few months, I find myself no longer feeling alone. The emptiness that was in my heart is shrinking and I'm finding joy once more in the little things in my life. I would be lying if I said that didn't scare me. I know what it means. I'm forgetting her. I'm letting her go. I'm letting her die and I'm not ready for that, not yet.

I need the pain and the sadness to remind myself of what I've lost but at the same time, I know in doing so I'm letting her down. She wouldn't want me to stop living and to wallow in her absence. She would want me to feel the loss and pain of it but to keep going. So, the question is how do I do that?

I want to be happy and feel alive again, but without her here to share that with me it feels wrong somehow like I'm putting her in my past, leaving her in a room, closing the door, and walking away. I can't let myself forget about her. I won't.

And what about Monica?

Last night was the most at peace I've felt since before the phone call I received all those weeks ago and it was all because of Monica. I've been trying to hide it, push it down, ignore it but something shifted last night. She's been there for me every step of the way. She's shared in my pain, understood my anger and outbursts and never once walked away. She took over at the restaurant, so I didn't need to worry about something else other than getting my head right again. Not only did she take care of me, but thanks to her the restaurant is thriving.

Feeling anything for anyone right now feels wrong. It's too soon. I can't let these feelings surface, especially not for Monica. Jane knew her, liked her. How would she feel if anything ever happened between us?

No.

You can't.

Jane is gone and she's not coming back, I've accepted that, but it's only been a few months since she died and it's too soon.

"Sam."

I turn around fast to see Monica standing behind me.

"Are you OK?"

Startled, I stumbled over my words. "I'm-how-what are you doing here?"

Hurt flashes across her face but just as fast as it's there it's gone again. "I knocked a few times and rang the bell and when you didn't answer I got worried. I tried the knob, and it was unlocked so I walked in. I continued to call for you, but you didn't answer so I searched the house until I found you."

"Oh. I'm sorry. I was," I paused rubbing my jaw. "Thinking. Must have been lost in thought. Why-why are you here, is everything alright?"

"I guess that depends on how you look at it."

I feel my eyebrows meet in the middle of my face.

"I had this really weird dream last night."

"What about?"

She starts to make her way across the bedroom to the window next to the bed. "It was about us."

"Oh, I." My hand finds its way to the back of my neck as the sweat forms.

"And Jane."

My heart skips a beat.

"She came to me in my dream last night."

"What do you mean?"

"I've heard stories about how the dead try to communicate with us after they are gone. To let us know they are still here and thinking about us and they are ok. I never thought I would be someone who had such an experience."

"Monica, you're not making any sense."

"In my dream, we were walking on the beach, just like last night. Except... we were holding hands."

I shove my hands in my pajama pockets. "Oh."

She turns slowly around to look at my expression, evaluating me. "Then, I heard her."

"Jane?"

She nods.

"What did she say?"

"She told me that you felt what I felt and that she wanted us to be together, that she gave us her blessing."

Before I can stop it, a laugh escapes from between my lips. "Monica, do you hear what you're saying?"

"I know it sounds crazy." The hurt vibrates in every word.

"It was only a dream. Last night was intense. It's expected."

"I thought so too but, Sam, I'm telling you it felt different. I knew it was Jane. I could even smell her perfume."

"You can make anything up in your dreams."

She shakes her head. "No, Sam. I smelled her perfume...in my room when I woke up."

My legs falter. I reach out my hand to rest it on the wall closest to me. I lean my body against it. "How..."

"I don't know. I thought I was imagining it. Maybe I only thought I smelled it from the dream, but it didn't go away."

"How is this possible? Why would she come to you, why wouldn't she come to me? And why now?"

"She said that you were afraid, afraid that feeling what you are feeling will make you forget her. She told me I had to come here and..."

"And what?"

"And" She releases a long sigh, "tell you how I feel. She said it couldn't wait. That if we waited, if I waited, it would give you time to talk yourself out of it. She wanted me to tell you you're ready and that you need to continue living your life."

"It's too soon."

She crossed the room to my side and hesitated before reaching up to take my hand in hers. "It's not too soon to admit there is something here, that we feel something for one another. I'm not saying we need to act on it, not yet. You need more time and I understand and I'm willing to wait for you, Sam. I'm willing to be here for you, whatever you need. But I also need you to know I love you. I've loved you for a long time and when you're ready, if you are ever ready, I'm willing to give this a shot, to see if we could have something. I would never try to take Jane's place and I never will. I want us to talk about her, always. Without her, neither of us would be who we are or where we are today, and we never would have met. I want to honor her memory, not shut it out."

Surprised and relieved, I reply, "I don't know what to say."

"You don't have to say anything. I just wanted you to know I'm here and I needed you to know how I felt. We are too young to stop living."

"I agree."

Kiss her, Sam.

I stop myself from jumping out of my skin as I look around the room frantically. Jane.

"Sam. Are you OK?"

"I'm…yes. I'm fine."

She squeezes my hand lightly. "I should go. I just wanted to check in on you and well, tell you." She smiles up at me before releasing my hand.

Without thinking I grab at hers tightly. She stops and turns to look me in the eyes. I can see in hers what I know I feel in mine. I know what she wants because I want it to, I feel it as she does, but I'm afraid to act on it. So many questions taking over. What if it's too soon? What if I can't be for her what she deserves? What if I can't open up to her? What if I forget Jane?

You won't.

Jane. In my head. I know it's her, but how?

Monica places her free hand on my chest tapping it lightly as she stands on her tippy toes and pecks me on the cheek. "I'll see you tonight."

She lowers herself back down and removes her hand from my chest as she starts to walk away, her hand still in mine. I push everything from my mind and act.

Be in the moment.

This moment.

I pull her gently till she's facing me once more. Her mouth opens, ready to speak but before she can get a word out, I place my hand on the back of her neck and pull her closer to me. I lean down until I feel our lips touch.

The uncertainty radiates off us both the moment our lips collide. Hesitation is clear and expected but to my surprise, it only lasts a moment. Her arms slowly come to wrap themselves around my now sweaty neck.

Should this feel like this? Feel OK?

Her lips soft against mine send chills down my spine. I never thought I would be able to do this, not to Monica, not to anyone for a long while. But hearing Jane, having her tell me to do it, made it feel right. I wanted to kiss Monica for the last few days but never wanted to act on it for more reasons than I care to admit.

What does this mean? What happens now?

There's no going back from this point. That's the only thing I know for sure at this moment.

Moving on

Jane

Looking on at Sam and Monica, my heart skips a beat but not in the way I would have expected. Seeing them together makes me happy, and peaceful. The last few weeks here I have felt a change in myself, almost like I am becoming used to this new normal, like I am not forgetting my life on earth but moving on from it, past it.

The closer I see Sam come to terms with life without me, the closer he gets to that place of peace, the closer I seem to be doing the same. But it's more than that. This life feels different than my old one. More like they are two different lifetimes. I feel less sadness and loss to the life I lived once.

I feel like I should be upset or mad about the change, but I cannot. I knew this was coming and I knew I had to do it for Sam and for myself. I know it's better this way. But above all, I know we will see each other again one day. I have faith and now, so does Sam.

I would not have picked anyone different to help him get through this time and his new life. I know she will take care of him and keep him on the right path so that when his time is over, he will meet me here.

As I let the picture of them intertwined slip from behind my eyes, I feel the last bit of weight on my shoulders lift. I open my eyes slowly as a smile forms on my face. Life without seeing Sam every day was not one I had ever entertained but now that it's my reality, for the first time, I feel OK with it. I have plenty here to do and keep my days and nights full and now so does Sam.

"Jane?"

I follow the sound of Jacob's voice until my eyes come to rest on his head poking through the opening in my door.

"Hey, Jacob, what's up?"

He smiles and pushes the door open the rest of the way. As he slowly lets himself inside, I see a stack of folders in his right hand. I motion to the objects in question as I sit up slowly in my bed.

"What are those?"

He glances down at the folders. "I was wondering if maybe you would like to help me welcome some new people today?"

Sitting up in my bed, I look at him with a look of surprise. "Really? Do you think I'm ready for that?"

"We've come a long way in such a short time, and I have learned something very important about you in the last few months."

"Which is?"

His smile widens, taking up the rest of his cheek space. "That you like to help people. That you'll do anything you can to help someone in need of it."

"And?"

He looks at the folders once more. "And that's what these people need. They need your help."

Understanding hits hard. "They will feel like I did when I first got here."

He nods.

"Scared, alone, and confused."

"Yes."

I do not need to think about what he's asking because I already know it's something I'm going to do. When I first arrived here, I was angry and alone. I could not understand this place or what it really meant. Heaven is something people talk and know about but when you get here, it's still a mystery. Still, something doesn't feel right. Remembering how I felt and knowing where I am now makes me happy to be able to help anyone I can.

I look at him and smile. "You came to the right girl."

"I knew I did."

* * *

Meeting the newcomers was not as hard as I expected. It reminded me of the first day I got here feeling dazed and confused but unsure and scared, all wrapped into one. I felt alone and all I wanted was to return home. Seeing the newbies made me realize how far I have come and how much my life has changed. It also made me more confident in my ability to help them since I had been in their shoes only a few short months ago.

Life here was something different, to say the least but it was peaceful and it was nice knowing I still had a purpose. I was able to help those who were scared and unsure of where to go and what would happen once they got here. I was still able to make a difference. In the end for me, all that matters is that Sam is happy and living his life once more, but also that I can still find a way to help people.

Sarah, one of the newcomers, was young like me. I knew she would need the most help to come to accept what happened and I knew I was the one for the job. I had helped Sam and now it was time to help those who needed me more. I would still check in on him from time to time to make sure he was doing ok and because I still missed my best friend, but at the end of the day, I knew my job was done. He had Monica and she had him, just as it was meant to be, just as God had intended.

I pull myself from my thoughts as I look over at the clock sitting on my nightstand and jump out of bed.

"I'm late!"

I throw my slippers on my feet, begging for protection from the cool floor tiles. I open my bedroom door to find Sarah on the other side, right hand raised ready to knock, and a shy smile on her face.

"I wasn't sure if I should knock or wait."

I smile at her in apology for my tardiness. "I'm sorry I lost track of time." I bring the door home and turn to face her. "Also, don't ever be afraid to knock. I'm always here and if I'm running late a knock is always a nice kick in the butt to get me in gear."

Sarah laughs lightly. A sweet, shy laugh that reminds me of what late-night girl hangouts used to be like as a teen, sleepovers with your best friends as you watched movies and made each other laugh as you stayed up way past the time you should have, only to wake groggy in the morning.

I smiled at the memory. "Today I thought we would take things slow. I will show you around so you know where everything is and maybe we can share a little bit about each other. How does that sound?"

She nods her head in agreement. "I would like that."

We walk the hall in silence for a few moments before Sarah's low voice breaks through the still air around us.

"I'm happy you were assigned to me."

I peer over at her as she looks down at the floor.

"I am too. I feel it will be a good match for both of us."

She turns her attention to me. "Really?"

"Yes. See, I got here not too long ago myself and I had a hard time coming to terms with what happened and what I felt I lost."

"Do...did you feel like you got let down, or screwed out of something that should have been yours?"

I nod.

"I don't like feeling this way and I'm trying to understand and accept it, but I'm finding that hard to do."

"I won't sugarcoat things for you. It is going to take some time but once you get to that place and you find peace...this place becomes more than a home for you. You start to see that this is where you were always meant to be. That our lives back on earth were only a stop along the way."

"Makes sense."

"I don't know if you are religious or not, not everyone who finds their way to heaven needs to be all about God as He is all forgiving and loves all His children, but I always was and when I first got here, I was more than angry with him but now I understand. This was my path to walk down and at the end of it I am still happy here. That is all that God wants for us, his children, in the end is to find peace and be happy and I would say with certainty that that is what you will find here. Just give it some time."

Sarah stops in her place and rests her hand on my arm making me come to a stop as I turn to look back at her.

"I want to thank you, Jane. For everything. For being open with me and honest and for sharing how you felt when you first arrived compared to now. It really means a lot and makes things...easier. I was worried about leaving, not so much my life but my loved ones."

"I more than understand."

She looks hard into my eyes like she is searching for something in them.

"Did you...who did you leave behind? If you don't mind me asking."

"My husband."

Her mouth forms in an O shape as the surprise spreads through the rest of her face.

"You were married?"

I nod.

"But you're so young."

"Yes. Well, like they say, when you know you know, right?"

"I'm sorry that came off as judgmental. I didn't mean anything by it."

"I know. Don't worry, it takes a lot more than that to offend me."

"Thank God for that because my tongue tends to be a lot faster than my brain."

I laugh lightly. "I know what you mean. I used to be the same way."

"If you don't mind me asking...how did you deal? Leaving your husband behind, I mean?"

"I worried about it, stressed over how he would cope and, me being me, I had to find a way to make sure he was ok and taken care of before I could focus on myself here."

115

"Understandable. But how did you do that? If that's ok to ask."

I shrug. "No biggie to me. I learned how to reach out to him. He couldn't see me really, but I … intervened, I guess is the right word."

"Intervened? How?"

"Little things, really, but all that matters was at the end, he found his path again and he's happy and living his life which is what I wanted for him."

"It must be hard."

I smile lightheartedly, "Which part?"

"Letting him go. Both of you being without the other and having to move on with life…if that's what we call this."

"It was at first. I saw the pain he was in and that was the hardest thing for me. I knew there was nothing I could do to make that pain go away. I could not go back to him. So, I did what I needed to, to help him fill in the emptiness."

"What did you do?"

I sigh, hoping she won't think I'm officially crazy after this. "I put him in the path of a mutual friend."

"You mean…" She paused in surprise.

"Yes."

"Wow. I…I don't think I would be able to do that."

"You would be surprised what you are capable of once you're put in a position. It was about him, not me."

"That's amazing. I'm glad it was you they paired me with. Having someone like you as my guide will make this transition easier for me, I think."

"That's my hope."

An amazing surprise

Sam

OK, just do it. It's time, there is nothing wrong with asking her. It's been a year and you have known each other forever.

Just do it.

You got this.

"Monica."

Her loving eyes meet mine and my thoughts fly away.

"Sam." She says my name playfully.

"I...um...so our anniversary is coming up."

Her smile widens across her face. "I know. It's hard to believe it's already been a year."

"It feels like so much longer than that."

She turns her attention back towards me. "Yes. Yes, it does."

"I...I wanted to take you somewhere nice tonight to celebrate."

She knocks me off guard when she says, "I have a better idea."

"Oh...what would that be?"

She takes my hand in hers pulling me along slowly. "I think we should go to the restaurant."

"But we're there almost every day. You deserve something better than that for our anniversary dinner."

"It's where things changed with us. It's where we first started this. Plus, we should be proud of what we have achieved together in this last year. Opening not one but three other restaurants and expanding this one and the fact that none have gone under but instead thrived. Not one, but all of them. We have so much to celebrate, and it all starts with the business. I would love to celebrate there."

I find myself smiling back at her in awe. "How did I get so lucky?"

"We both did."

She stops abruptly, turning to face me and before I have time to react her lips are against mine brushing them softly. She pulls back, looks me in the eyes, and smiles.

"So, it is settled then."

Confused, it takes me a moment to realize what she's talking about. "Oh, yes. If you want to go to the restaurant, then the restaurant it is."

She lowers herself back down on the balls of her feet and pulls me along, my hand still in hers. "Good."

"I'll call Robert and set it up for tonight."

"I might have to meet you there. I have something I need to do in an hour."

I looked down at her in surprise. "Oh, really?" I ask playfully.

"Yes, really. And no I'm not telling you what it is."

"Oh, man. I guess my charm and powers of persuasion are waning."

"Honey, those powers never worked on me anyway."

"Oh, really now?"

She looks back at me and I see the playfulness growing in her eyes. "Yes, really."

She lets go of my hand and starts to make a run for it. I smile and give chase. Taking small steps, giving her a chance to get away.

Until…

I spring into action and within three normal strides, I am on her. She starts to scream and giggle which I love so much as my arms go around her and pull her close. My lips resting at her ear as she begins to calm down in my arms.

I whisper in her ear. "I love you, Monica."

She whispers back. "I love you, Sam."

* * *

I walk through the restaurant door to see the lights down low. Candles and lilies are on the table in the center of the room. Red and pink roses on all the other tables, just as I asked Robert to do.

"Boss."

"Robert. How many times do I need to ask you to call me by my name?"

He smiles. "Just one more time, boss."

I chuckle lightly. "One of these days I'm going to get you to stop calling me that."

He grins at me knowingly, "I suppose we will see."

"Yes, we will."

Robert looks around the room while saying, "Everything is ready."

I slap my hand on his back. "Thank you, my friend."

"Jackson and Raven will be your servers and Carlos demanded to be the cook for tonight's event." He says with a smile.

"Thank you. Your work is done. Go home and see your family."

"Thank you, boss."

I grunt and say to him as he heads for the front doors. "No, thank you. Have a wonderful night."

"You too, boss." He says the last word with formality as he smiles. I strain to hear his next words, hand on the door ready to make his exit. "Jane would be so proud of you."

He turns and walks away as my heart is left pounding in my chest.

Jane.

It has been so long without her and if it hadn't been for Monica, I don't know if I ever would have found my way again. I know Jane would be happy for us, and that alone makes me know I am living the right way and making the right choices. Not a day that goes by that I don't think about or miss her, but I know I'll see her again and when I do, I'll have so much to share with her.

I remember a conversation we once had, about if something ever happened to one of us, we both told each other that we wanted whoever got left behind to continue living. Don't be sad, for we would be together again, and no matter what, we wanted them to be happy and to live so that there would be so much to share when we were reunited. I have no doubt in my mind that if roles were reversed, I would be happy for her. So, I know she is smiling down at me as happy as I am.

"Sam."

I turn back towards the door to see Monica looking around the restaurant in awe. However, I'm the one who is mesmerized. She looks beautiful in the dress she is wearing. It stops at her knees, hugging and showing off all her curves. The color is beautiful as it sits against her skin. Midnight blue. The straps resting down the sides of her shoulders and her hair is pinned up along her head.

"How…"

"Robert," I say with a smile.

She looks down shyly. "Of course."

"You look radiant."

She peers up at me with a smile on her face. "You don't look so bad yourself, stud."

She walks slowly across the room to my side. I take her hand in mine and usher her to our table, pull out her seat and when she is seated, I push it in for her. I make my way to mine and once I'm settled her smile grows.

"So where did you run off to today?"

"You'll know soon enough."

Raven and Jackson exit the kitchen and come to our table. Raven smiles at me but her smile widens when she looks at Monica. "You look beautiful."

"Thank you, Raven, and thank you for working tonight."

She looks over at Jackson. "It's our pleasure." She nudges his arm with her elbow. "Right, Jackson."

"Yes. We are happy to be here."

Monica suppresses a giggle. "We will make sure you have all next weekend off. How does that sound?"

Jackson smiles and stands up straight. "Thank you so much, Monica."

"No. Thank you."

Raven and Jackson return to the kitchen as Monica rearranges the dishware in front of her making room for a notebook she pulled from her purse without me noticing.

"And what might that be?"

She peers up at me with a sheepish smile on her face. "I figured since we have a few moments..."

I place my hand up in protest. "Monica. No. No work tonight."

"But."

"No. Tonight we celebrate. Tomorrow we can continue with business, deal?"

Her smile expands over the rest of her face. "Fine. You win."

She returns the notebook, unopened, to its home in her beige purse.

"What are you getting for dinner tonight?"

I take a sip from the perspiring glass in front of me. I smile at her as I swallow the cool contents.

"Let me guess. The usual?"

I shake my head.

"Something new? Now this I have to see."

"I figured it's a special night so I should change it up a little bit."

She folds her arms over her chest in a playful manner as the smile on her face widens in interest.

"OK. I'll bite."

"I was thinking of the Parmesan Risotto with the cooked shrimp."

Her mouth opens in a big 'o' shape.

"What?"

"Nothing. I'm just surprised. You've never liked those kinds of dishes before."

"I figured maybe I should try it. After all, it is one of your favorites. There has to be a reason and I would like to know what's so appealing about it."

Leaning her elbows on the table, she folds her arms over themselves as she looks at me sweetly.

"Well, if you don't like it, I don't want to hear about it, OK?"

I grin. "Deal."

She straightens up and sits back in her chair looking at the kitchen.

"I thought they would have been back by now to take our order."

I reach for my glass before answering, "I took the liberty of ordering for you." I place the glass to my nervous dry lips once more.

She looks at me in shock. "What?"

I swallow. "I figured I knew what you liked, and I thought it would be nice for us to enjoy the dish together."

"Oh, did you now?"

The corner of her lip moves up into a half smile.

"I could cancel the order if you like." I smile at her devilishly.

"Oh, no, that's perfectly fine." She says in a playful sarcastic tone. "I'm sure I'll enjoy it just as much tonight as I normally do."

"Maybe more so." I take another swig.

Monica looks at me like she is anticipating something. She knows something more is going on.

"Sam."

"Hmm."

"You are acting funny."

I return the glass to its home on the table. "Am I?"

She nods. "Spill it."

"I don't know what you mean."

"Something is going on. Just tell me."

The kitchen doors swing open as Jackson emerges with a plate in each hand. He lowers one dish down in front of Monica and the other in front of me.

Smiling he says, "Enjoy."

He walks away.

I pick up my fork ready to dig in.

"Oh, no you don't."

"I almost forgot. Of course." I close my eyes and fold my hands together, "Thank you Father for this beautiful food, the life you have given me, and of course, for my gorgeous partner without whom this life would have still been merely a dream. Amen."

"That's not what I meant."

"It wasn't?"

Her right eyebrow goes up and almost meets her hairline. I suppress a smile.

"Sam. For real. What's going on?"

"Eat your meal before it gets cold."

She leans back in her seat and stares at me.

"I promise after we eat, I'll tell you."

"Fine."

"Fine."

Eating is harder than I thought it would be. My nerves have my stomach all knotted up, but I do my best. In a matter of minutes, I will have my answer to the most important question I could ever ask her. I stand up and grab my plate. I turn to the kitchen.

"I'll be right back."

Before she can say a word, I'm behind the doors breathing hard. I take in a slow breath and look over at Raven.

"Is it ready?"

She nods.

"Ok. I'm going to walk back out and as soon as I sit down, bring it out, ok?"

"You got it, boss."

I turn around and push the doors open once more. I walked over to the table faster than I thought. I force myself down in my seat, nerves starting to take over completely as beads of sweat form on my forehead.

"Sam. Are you alright?"

"I'm fine."

"You're sweating."

"I'm a little hot. Are you hot?"

She shakes her head no and before she can get out another word, Raven and Jackson emerge from the kitchen once more. Raven places a beautiful chocolate cupcake with vanilla frosting down in front of Monica. However, she continues to look at me with a worried expression, completely unaware of the 14-karat white gold diamond ring sitting on top of the cupcake's frosting.

I stand up and make my way to her side of the table as Raven and Jackson move to stand at the bar, not wanting to miss my humiliation. I get down on one knee as I take Monica's hand in mine. Shock, surprise, and uncertainty are clear on her face and features as I feel her hand tense in mine.

"This past year you have been more than a friend to me. You helped me overcome the hardest time of my life with just grace, patience, and understanding. You helped me build this wonderful world, my dream. You made this reality possible for not only me but us. You are my best friend, my partner and without you, your love, patience, understanding and guidance, I don't know where I would be today. You are the most passionate and creative person I know, and you don't have a selfish bone in your body. You make sure every day that I never forget Jane and because of that, it only makes me love you more, makes my heart grow bigger. I don't ever want to lose you." I reach over to the cupcake and gently take the ring off the top. I clean it off with the sleeve of my shirt. "Monica, will you do me the honor and make me the happiest man on earth by becoming my wife?"

A small sob escapes her lips as she gets up from her seat and throws her arms around my neck holding me tight, her lips against my eye as she answers in a sob.

"Yes. Yes, Sam. I would love to marry you."

Happy For Them

⸙

Jane

I smile as I see Jacob coming down the hall in my direction.

"Good morning."

"Good morning to you. Big day today." He says with an unsure smile plastered across his face.

Over the last year here I've gotten to know Jacob well enough to tell his different facial expressions and I know the reason for the one he is currently wearing.

"Yes. Yes, it is."

"How are you feeling about it?"

"Honestly."

He nods.

"I'm happy," I reply as a genuine smile forms on my face.

"Really?"

"Yes. I couldn't be happier for them."

"Well, that's good at least. Shows how far you've come. Although even when you first arrived here, I never got the feeling you were jealous or not wanting Sam to move on. It was always more of the opposite."

"When you love someone, that's how it should be. It would have been selfish of me to act differently than I did."

"True. But even then, not many people can put someone they love before themselves. We all talk a good game but not many of us can walk it. However, you, you amaze me."

My smile falters in a playful way, "I hope you mean in a good way."

His smile widens across his clean-shaven face as a chuckle rumbles in his chest. "Of course. I've never met anyone like you and I'm so happy that I was able to be your guide and have the chance to meet someone as selfless as you. The world needs more people like you in it."

"I always said if people could be more selfless, help those less fortunate, even if they only to give a little of themselves, if everyone did it the world would be a much better place because of it. After all, giving an hour of your time once a month to help at a soup kitchen or giving canned goods and groceries to churches to help feed the hungry goes a long way. Even twenty dollars a week in some sort of donation. If everyone could do these things, even one of them, I know the world would be a much better place. I always hoped to see us get there one day. Who knows? Maybe one day we will."

"And you'll have the best view in the house when that day comes."

I turn to him with joy and hope in my heart. "I can't wait."

"So…will you be watching in on today's event?"

I nod.

"Would you mind some company?"

"Not at all." I feel my grin take over my face, grateful for the company.

As happy as I am for Sam and Monica, it still hurts seeing him move on and continue to live the life we were meant to have. However, I would not change a thing and I couldn't be happier that they have one another for, what I hope, is the rest of their lives.

Sam is so nervous standing at the altar, just like on our wedding day. Not much has changed it seems. I smile as the wedding party makes their way down the aisle and soon after Monica makes her entrance. She is stunning and I'm so happy these two will have one another after today.

Tears form in my eyes as they exchange their vows and when the priest announces his final line Sam and Monica kiss, sending the room into an uproar of excitement. I can't stop myself from grinning ear to ear as I watch them embrace one another and I know in my heart they are going to be ok.

Wedding Day

❦

Sam

I can't remember the last time I was this nervous. My hands have never been so sweaty as I stand up on the altar as the wedding music sounds through the church. I feel the moisture forming on my hands.

What if she changed her mind?

What if she doesn't come and leaves me standing up here?

Stop.

I try to pull myself together but with no luck. The fact that she agreed to marry me still amazes me. Monica is one of the most amazing women I've ever met. Anyone would be lucky to have her, and I guess on some level I'm having a hard time figuring out why she chose me. I'm more than blessed to have her in my life, but to have her as my soon-to-be wife feels like a dream. Without her, my life wouldn't be what it is today. Honestly, I don't think I ever would have made it out of my grief without her, let alone have my restaurant thriving like it is. She is amazing in every sense of the word and I'm the luckiest man to have such a talented, beautiful and thoughtful woman like her by my side.

Lost in my head, I barely notice everyone stand and look to the back of the church. I glance down the aisle to see the bridesmaids and flower girl making their way in my direction, but no sign of Monica yet. When the last person starts to walk, I feel my stomach flip until my eyes come to rest on her.

She's stunning.

Never has she looked more beautiful than at this moment. Her shoulder-length fawn hair lays beautifully on her bare shoulders. Her beautiful white dress hangs off her shoulders and the train drapes behind her in a perfect white trail. The bodice of her wedding dress hugs her curves down to her hips and then it fans out in all directions around her. The exquisite lavender arrangement in her hands adding only to the lovely dress and the even more gorgeous woman wearing it. The sequins only add to its beauty, and they complement the veil that is covering Monica's face from my view.

I am breathless.

As she makes her way up the aisle my heart pounds loudly in my chest and it takes everything in me to stand where I am and not run to meet her.

She is here.

She is mine.

I am hers.

In mere moments this amazing woman will become my wife and I will be able to spend the rest of my life with her.

Planning.

Loving.

But most of all, living.

How did I get so lucky? To not only have one, but two beautiful, smart, caring and life-changing women in my life, to lose one only to gain another. I always believed you get one, one person to love and share your life with, one soul mate. Many people never get to find that one person in their life to make them feel whole, make them the best person they can be, and feel like they have someone in their corner no matter what.

Me?

I got two.

We meet everyone for a reason, I've never doubted that. But when you lose something so precious that it changes your life entirely and you never feel you'll find your way to the surface again, only to be pulled out by the hands of someone you never expected, God knew what he was doing. At this moment, I do not doubt that this was the path all of us were meant to live, to have each other and grow together and become who we were meant to be, only to end up where God had planned all along.

I do not doubt that Jane is watching over me and that she had a part in bringing Monica and me together. She knew we needed each other and for her, that was enough.

Finally, she reaches my side and comes to stand in front of me. I smile facing her as I reach out and lift her veil over her head to see her shy smile is a mirror of my own and for the first time, my heart and stomach are calm. My thoughts, the world, everyone in the pews, it all falls away and all I see is her.

The priest brings me back as he begins, "Dearly beloved, you have come together into the house of the Church so that in the presence of the Church's minister and the community, your intention to enter into Marriage may be strengthened by the Lord with a sacred seal. Christ abundantly blesses the love that binds you. Through a special Sacrament, He enriches and strengthens those He has already consecrated by Holy Baptism, that they may be faithful to each other forever and assume all the responsibilities of married life. And so, in the presence of the Church, I ask you to state your intentions. Sam and Monica, have you come here to enter into Marriage without coercion, freely and wholeheartedly?"

"I have." Monica and I say in unison and smile at one another.

"Are you prepared, as you follow the path of marriage, to love and honor each other for as long as you both shall live?"

We look in each other's eyes as we say together, "I am."

"Are you prepared to accept children lovingly from God and to bring them up according to the law of Christ and his Church?"

Monica replies, "I am."

"I am."

"Since it is your intention to enter the covenant of Holy Matrimony, join your right hands, and declare your consent before God and His Church."

We join our right hands as the priest gestures to me to continue.

I smile at Monica as I say to her, "I, Sam, take you, Monica, to be my wife. I promise to be faithful to you, in good times and in bad, in sickness and in health, to love you and to honor you all the days of my life."

"I, Monica, take you, Sam, to be my husband. I promise to be faithful to you, in good times and in bad, in sickness and in health, to love you and to honor you all the days of my life."

The priest turns in my direction, "Sam, do you take Monica to be your wife? Do you promise to be faithful to her in good times and in bad, in sickness and in health, to love her and to honor her all the days of your life?"

"I do."

"Monica, do you take Sam to be your husband? Do you promise to be faithful to him in good times and in bad, in sickness and in health, to love him and to honor him all the days of your life?"

"I do."

"May the Lord in His kindness strengthen the consent you have declared before the Church and graciously bring to fulfillment his blessings within you. What God has joined, let no one put asunder. May the God of Abraham, the God of Isaac, the God of Jacob, the God who joined together our first parents in paradise, strength and bless in Christ the consent you have declared before the Church, so that what God joins together, no one may put asunder. Let us bless the Lord."

Everyone replies, "Thanks be to God."

The priest looks to the rings as he continues, "Bless and sanctify your servants in their love, O Lord, and let these rings, a sign of their faithfulness, remind them of their love for one another, through Christ our Lord."

In unison, we reply, "Amen."

He then sprinkles the rings. When finished, he hands one to me and one to Monica before turning back to me.

I take Monica by the hand as I begin to place the ring on her finger with trembling hands and a smile on my face. "Monica, receive this ring as a sign of my love and fidelity. In the name of the Father, and of the Son, and of the Holy Spirit."

Smiling, Monica takes my hand and places the ring on my finger as she recites the following, "Sam, receive this ring as a sign of my love and fidelity, in the name of the Father, and of the Son, and of the Holy Spirit."

"I now pronounce you husband and wife; you may kiss the bride."

I pull her close as a warmth begins to spread up my arms through my body. A simple touch makes me feel at peace, and calm, like this is where I am meant to be. I move closer until our lips touch lightly and the world falls away.

Repeating conversations

Jane

"How are you doing?" Jacob asks.

I smile. "I'm great."

"You sure?"

I place a reassuring hand on his forearm. "Really. I'm fine. I'm happy for Sam and Monica. I wouldn't have it any other way."

"You have come a long way."

I remove my hand as my smile spreads wider. "Thank you, and so you keep saying," I say sarcastically.

"I'm sorry. I didn't mean it the way I think you are taking it."

I chuckle. "I know you didn't."

"Sorry, I keep repeating myself. I'm just happy to see you…accepting this new life."

"You know, I always wondered…" I trail off.

"What?"

"I always wondered what it was like for the people that died. Like, how they felt or what they went through when they left. I knew how hard it would be to lose someone and be the one left behind, so I understood what Sam would be going through, but I never knew what to expect from this side of things."

Jacob looks off into the room full of people. "In some ways, it's easier for us. We have this," he gestures to the room. "We have peace, and feel nothing but love and contentment once we move beyond our lives on earth. This is meant to be the end, our end but also our beginning, a place where no one gets sick, everyone feels loved and happy. We get the good end of the deal. Those left behind must grieve and live life without the person they loved and lost. They have to find a way to keep living."

I nod in agreement.

"I like that even after we are gone and find peace here that we can still see the ones we left behind. We know they are ok. That only adds to the peace here. At least for me, it does."

"For me too," I say with an encouraging smile.

"So, Sarah should be here any minute now. What's on the agenda today?"

"Welcoming some more new members. Every day there are more. I don't know how we have enough people to handle the meet and greet of everyone sometimes."

"God always makes sure everyone is taken care of. He knows who's best to place with who comes here to make the transition easier."

"I'm glad He paired me with you."

Jacob turns to face my direction. "Me too."

"Hey, guys."

We both turn to see Sarah walking at a fast pace in our direction. I smile. "Hey, Sarah."

"How long do we have?"

I glance at the clock in the far corner. "Should head to the entrance now. Should be here any time now."

Sarah glances in Jacob's direction. "Will you be joining us?" She asks with a shy smile.

No matter what anyone tells me, I think she likes Jacob and I've noticed over the last few weeks he seems to as well, but for some reason people are just as confusing here as our lives back on earth. Everyone still seems to be scared in some way.

I smile as I hold back a laugh and slap Jacob on the back. "Yeah, Jacob, will you be tagging along today?"

"I…I didn't see my name on the greeting list today."

"When has that ever stopped you before?" I say as I cross my arms over my chest.

He runs his hand through his hair before looking at Sarah shyly. "I guess I could tag along."

"Great. So, let's get going." I say as I grab Jacob and Sarah both by the forearm and move forward.

Two Becomes Three

<u>Three Years Later</u>

Sam

"It's time!" Monica's voice rings through my ears.

"You sure?"

I sit up fast from my sleeping place, letting the sleep fall away from my tired body.

"Yes."

"OK. OK. Um…you get your shoes on I'll grab everything." I yawn as I throw my legs down and my bare feet meet the cool floor.

The cold discards the last of the sleep that remained in me. I jump to my feet with a new energy as I grab Monica's shoes and place them at her feet. I reach for her coat and place it on her lap.

"It's chilly out," I say before running from the room.

I grab the two bags by the front door, and the keys, before I head out the front door. I throw the bags in the back of the chilly vehicle and put the key in and turn to start. I hear the engine purr to life and turn the dial to heat and exit the car.

I run back up the stairs just as Monica exits the bedroom with a pained smile on her face and one hand placed on her lower back while the other sits on her growing belly rubbing in a circular motion. She glances up at me as her smile grows. I reach my hands out for her.

"I got you," I say as I take her one hand in mine and place the other around her lower back.

We take one step at a time, slowly. By the time we make it to the car, it's toasty warm. I glance back as I put the car in reverse and back out of the drive. In ten minutes, we reach our destination.

The hospital.

* * *

"What can I do?" I asked the nurse.

"Keep her company and apply cool compresses to her head, chest, and neck. It will help."

I nod as she exits the room once more.

"How are you feeling?" Not knowing what else to say.

She looks at me with pain etched in every line of her face.

"Like this baby is ready to come out." She laughs with great effort.

"What can I do? Tell me what I can do to help, please."

She places her hand on mine squeezing it lightly. "Just be here."

I place my hand over hers feeling defeated as I whisper. "Always."

* * *

"It's time. Get ready to push when we tell you." The nurse says.

I stand next to Monica. Her face and hair covered in sweat. The pain has taken so much energy and life from her. For, not the first time in the last two days, I'm afraid. I'm worried about our child, and I'm worried about her. I know women do this every day and this is the process, but seeing her in this kind of pain and not being able to do anything to help, knowing that the human body can only take so much before the heart gives out, seeing all the blood, I would be crazy if I wasn't concerned.

"Push."

Monica squeezes my hand so tight that our hands turn white. She bares her teeth as her upper back lifts off the bed as she begins to push.

"Relax." The nurse says.

Monica's back falls back to the bed as her eyes close and she takes in a breath. I reach up with my free hand to move the sweat-soaked hair off her sticky forehead. I continue to rub her forehead with my finger in a reassuring gesture.

"Push."

Monica repeats the same actions until the nurse, once more tells her to relax. We repeat this several times.

"I see the head. Keep pushing, you're almost there, Monica," The doctor and nurse say.

I can see the energy draining from Monica faster now.

Through shallow breaths, I hear her say, "I can't, I'm too tired. I can't push anymore."

"You need to. We need you to push right now," the doctor says frantically.

I lean down close to her. "You can do this, honey. You are so close. A few more good pushes and you will have our baby girl in your arms. You can do it."

She turns her head in my direction and I see the light come back to her eyes and I know it's my words she needed. She looks back to the doctor, lifts her back off the bed once more, and bares her teeth as she pushes.

"OK. Rest for a moment."

She falls back to the bed.

"OK. Again."

I squeeze her hand as she repeats the process three more times.

"Last push, make it a good one."

Monica bears down and gives it everything she has. Next thing I know, I see the nurse walking away with something small in her arms.

"OK, Monica. Relax, honey," The doctor says.

Monica closes her eyes as I apply a cool rag to her forehead.

"Is she…is she OK?" She asks in a low, exhausted tone.

"I'll go check."

I walk away and head to the station where the nurse is working on our little girl.

"Is she…"

The nurse turns around to face me with a little body in her arms.

"She looks healthy. We are going to go place her on your wife's chest now. Skin-to-skin contact is important right after birth."

She moves past me to my wife's side as I follow behind. Monica's eyes open and a smile forms as our daughter is placed on her chest. Her arm reaches up to hold her in place as her eyes find mine and her smile grows even bigger as a slight sob escapes her lips.

I reach her side as I whisper, "You did it. She's beautiful."

She turns to me. "We did it."

I bend down and place a light kiss on her lips, then her forehead, and lastly, one on our daughter's forehead.

"You did amazing. She's amazing."

News

❧

Two years later

S am
"I have to head into the restaurant to make sure everything is set for tomorrow. Will you be ok here for a few hours with Faith?"

Monica smiles as Faith walks over to her mother's side with her new favorite blanket. It was mine when I was her age. My mother kept it all these years in hopes of passing it on to me when I had a child of my own, and I am happy she did. It was hand-knit by my great-grandmother when I was born. It is yellow and white.

"Mama. Up," Faith says as she lifts her hands in her pick-me-up gesture.

Monica smiles as she reaches down to pick her up. "I think we will be just fine."

I smile and lean down to kiss her lightly on the lips, and Faith on the forehead. "I'll be back soon."

"You better." She says with a playful smile.

* * *

"How's it looking, Robert?"

"All systems go."

"And the work schedule. Did they get out to everyone?"

Roberts nods. "Yes."

"OK good. I just need everything to run smoothly tomorrow."

"It will. I will make sure of it. You and Monica don't have to worry about anything here. I know Monica wanted tonight to go without interruption."

I look at him in confusion. "Tonight?"

"Oh, was I not supposed to say anything?"

"I don't know because I don't know what you're talking about."

Robert makes a gesture with his hand and lips like his lips are sealed. "I guess you'll have to go home and see."

"Thanks for nothing, Robert," I say with a smile on my face as I head for the exit.

"Anytime, sir." He smiles.

* * *

"Monica."

I walk in the front door to all the lights off, almost falling through the door.

"We're in here."

I head in the direction of our living room to see Monica and Faith sitting on the couch watching one of Faith's favorites, *Moana*. It has been one of the only ones to keep her attention since she was only 11 months old.

I glance around the room till my eyes come to rest on a gift bag. "Who's that for?"

Monica looks up and smiles at me. "You."

I smile back. "What's the occasion?"

"Have to open it to find out."

"It's almost Faith's bedtime, so how about I get her bottle and outfit all ready, and then we can pick out a movie to watch together as I open your gift?"

"That sounds like a nice plan. How were things at the restaurant?"

"Robert has everything handled."

"I knew he would."

I smile as I say, "Well, you are normally right."

"Trying to butter me up?" She asks with a chuckle.

I shake my head as I make my way to the kitchen.

"Bottle and bed ready," I say to Monica. I turn my attention to Faith. "Time for bed, Faithy. Let's get changed, kiddo."

She reaches her arms up. "Up. Dada. Up."

"I'll be right back. Say goodnight to Mama."

"Night night, Mama."

"Goodnight, my little monkey. Love you."

Heading up the stairs to tuck in Faith, her arms are wrapped around my neck and her head rests against my shoulder. Moments like this make my life feel full. I never knew what being a father would feel like. All I knew was I wanted kids one day. Now, I could not imagine a life without this little girl. I did not realize what my life was missing until she came along.

All the little things, her saying my name, reaching for me, her arms embracing me, and the way her face lights up when I enter the room, each one tugs at my heart in a big way, knowing that love is unconditional and that I would do anything to keep her safe and make her happy. I fear the day she grows up and stops being my little girl, the moment she realizes she doesn't need me anymore.

That will be my saddest day.

* * *

"All tucked in. Did you pick a movie?"

"Yup." She replies in a matter-of-fact tone, meaning whatever she picked I'm stuck watching.

"Oh, no. Don't tell me."

"Yup." She says with a mocking smile.

"Again?"

"Hey, I love this movie. And in some ways, it reminds me of us."

Surprised by her words, I ask, "How so?"

"It's how we used to be and where I hope we end up."

I sigh. "Fine, you win. We will watch it again." I drag out the last word.

"Say it."

"I don't remember the name."

"Yes, you do." She says playfully.

"Fine. We will watch the Nicholas Sparks movie The Choice for the millionth time this year."

"That's better."

We laugh as I take a seat next to her on the couch.

"Now, your gift."

I reach over to grab the bag while looking in her direction, "I wonder what it could be. My birthday isn't for a few more months."

I reach inside and pull out something wrapped up in tissue paper. I undo the tape as my eyes come to rest on a pregnancy test and onesies. I look over at Monica.

"Are."

She nods. "Yes."

I grab her tight and kiss her hard on the lips. "You're sure?"

"Yes. I took, like, four tests. I'm pregnant."

I look down at her stomach, placing a hand against it. "This is the best gift."

She leans over and kisses me softly.

"How far along are you?"

"I have an appointment set for next Wednesday."

"Ok. I'll make sure Robert can handle the restaurant for the day."

Looking at me knowingly she says, "You don't have-"

"Oh, yes I do. I'm going."

She pulls me in close for a tight hug. "Whoever thought our lives could be this good? God is great."

"Yes. Yes, he is." I say matter-of-factly.

* * *

Wednesday

"It looks like you're about six weeks in. Would you like to know the sex of the baby?"

Monica and I look at each other and smile. "Yes."

"Ok, you can do the blood test soon or you can wait a few more months. That's up to you."

"I think we will wait for the ultrasound at four months," Monica says.

"Ok. We will see you for your next appointment then. You can check out with the nurse up front on your way out. Congratulations."

"Thank you, doctor." We say together.

"I hope it's a boy," I replied.

"Sam." She says in her annoyed tone.

"What? We already have a girl, so a boy would be nice."

She faces forward before saying, "Yes. But I'll be happy as long as it's healthy."

"Me too. But I still want a boy." I say playfully.

"Come on you. Let's get home." She says with a chuckle.

Three Becomes Four

Three Months Later

S am

"You said you wanted to know the sex, correct?" The nurse asks as she prints out the ultrasound pictures.

Monica and I look at each other before looking back at the nurse as we nod.

"You're having a boy and so far, everything looks great. He's extremely healthy."

"A boy," I say.

"Yes, a boy," The nurse says with a smile.

I look at Monica. "Did you hear that?"

"Yes, Sam. I heard." She chuckles.

"We're having a boy and he's healthy." I pull her close for a hug. "God is great. I could not ask for more than this life I've been given. We are truly blessed."

"Yes, we are." She whispers.

"Faith is going to make an amazing big sister."

"It's going to be an adjustment for her, she's used to being the center of attention and the apple of your eye but yes she will be amazing."

I frown, "You really think it will be a problem?"

She smiles, "It's a given, children while young tend to get jealous, they love being the center of things. So, it's going to be different when a new baby is around and our attention has to be on him first and not her anymore."

I sigh, "She will be ok. We will make sure she is."

"I'm not worried." Monica smiles as she pulls her shirt back down over her growing stomach. "Well, let's go home and share the news with the little monkey."

Five Years Later

❧❧❧

Sam

I look to the heavens and whisper, "Thank you, Jane." I peer over my shoulder at my daughter, now seven years old and my son, already four years of age, playing catch with a worn-out old tether ball. "Thank you," I look into the bright white and blue sky one last time, "for everything." I smile before I turn around heading back towards my family.

"Who wanted to play catch?" I ask.

"Me, Daddy," Elijah says with such excitement.

"What about you, princess, do you want to join us?"

"I don't think so, Dad. Maybe I'll go help Mom in the kitchen for a bit."

"Daughter like mother, huh?" I smile, realizing a moment too late I said it backward.

"Nothing wrong with knowing how to cook, Dad."

"Hey, I never said there was," I say while placing my hands up in the air in a surrendering gesture.

"I want to be just like you and mom when I grow up. I want to run my own restaurant that has all my own recipes in it. I only want to cook when I want to."

"Which would be all the time." I chuckle.

"Again, I say nothing wrong with that, Dad."

"You're right." I turn to Elijah, "And what about you? What do you want to be when you get older?"

"I think I want to be an aminal vet person."

Faith chuckles. "You mean a veterinarian?"

Elijah smiles. "Yeah. That. I wanna be that, Daddy."

"Sounds like some good choices to me."

"But Dad." Faith starts. "Why would anyone want to be-"

I cut her off. "Because it's what your brother wants to be. Plus, just like everyone needs somewhere to eat and talk, someone also needs help taking care of their animals and the animals themselves need someone who cares enough about them to help."

I see the wheels turning in her head. "That makes sense and I do love animals or aminals as you call them, Elijah." She says with a smile. "Maybe we can do both together. Open a brother and sister restaurant and animal hospital."

"I like that," Elijah says with a smile.

"Good. Sounds like a plan, little brother." She says as she tosses the hair around on his head. "I'm going to head in and help mom now."

"I wanna help," Elijah says.

"Play catch with dad for a little while then you can come in and help me and mom. OK?"

"OK." He says with a smile before turning back in my direction.

How did I get so lucky?

Life could not be better. I have everything I have ever dreamed about. God blessed me in every way possible. Even when I strayed away from Him and His love and guidance, He never abandoned me. I could never be more grateful than I am at this moment.

"Thank you."

* * *

Jane

"Thank you, Jane," Sam says in a whisper before he looks back over his shoulder at his children, now four and seven years in age, playing catch, "thank you, for everything." He says with a smile before heading back inside with his family.

I smile back at him, happy to see him finally, wholly at peace and happy in his life. Knowing, senses he still thinks of me from time to time, missing me and what we could have had, but also knowing he is content in how his life turned out.

"That smile looks good on you." I hear Jacob's voice coming from the doorway behind me. "It's a great thing you've done for him, you know, and yourself in the process."

"It makes me happier than I can explain to see him this happy. He has a life he always wanted, and I couldn't be happier to see him finally have it. Plus, do you see how stinking cute those two are? They are going to go on and do amazing things, I can feel it."

"They are cute."

"You can say that again."

"They are cute." I turn around to see a smile on his face from ear to ear.

I chuckle.

Being here, dead, is not something I ever thought I would accept, let alone be happy about, but I am. I'm at peace. I am free and happy, and I got to reach the end of my journey sooner than most people do. I am no longer sad, angry, hurting, hungry, tired. I just am and one day everyone I love will be able to be here in this place with me and feel what I'm feeling, and I can't wait for them to experience this with me.

Everyone always talked about heaven, but no one ever really knew what it was or what to expect. I would be lying if I didn't say I was afraid to die because I was. I didn't know what would happen. I had faith, believed and trusted in God, and that I would be here one day and be at peace. But I never knew what to expect. I'm happy that God made me, made this, and that I was able to live the life I did before coming here. One thing no one was ever able to shake was my faith. Just because I didn't know for sure the answers to all my questions never meant I didn't believe in the end result or God or where I would end up. I trusted in Him and in life and death and everything He is and represents. Faith is a huge part of life and an even bigger part of death. Having it in life allows you peace in uncertain times. It guides you when you're unsure and it places a foundation at your feet to give you a basis on how a good person would live life. It allows you a connection to something that's in every living thing. Faith gives us God, a guide, a father, someone who's always there for us even though we can't see them.

When it comes to death, having faith allows you a sense of peace to know God is there waiting for you. He is making a place for you to live in peace for life after death.

Without faith, I don't know where I would be today, and I feel sad for those who can't or won't believe because they are missing out on the best parts of life and death, the unknown which gives us something no one could expect.

Faith gives us life and love everlasting, gives us a home.

About the Author

Laura Lukasavage started writing shortly after her mother's passing when she was only fourteen years old. She remembered how her mom would write 192 About the Author poems and letters to her stepdad and as a way to feel close to her mother she took up writing. She started with poems in eighth grade and short stories in high school. Once she started college in 2009 at Neumann University in Aston, PA her interest only grew. By the time she would transfer from Neumann to Rowan University in Glassboro, NJ in 2011, after her father's passing, is when she knew what her passions truly were. She majored in Radio, TV and Film productions with a minor in creative writing. She found her love of film and writing meshed together and this is where she felt at peace. Laura writes as a way to escape from reality but to also deal with life as a whole. She writes hoping that one day her books will be an escape for someone needing them just like the books she read in high school to escape the recent loss of her mother.

You can connect with me on:

🌐 https://publishingdreams20.wixsite.com/my-site

Also by Laura Lukasavage

Moonlight Secrets (Book 1)

Amberly's world is forever changed when she discovers she has the power to communicate with wolves telepathically. To learn how a witch can have this power Amberly embarks on a journey of self-discovery, world-altering love, and the truth about who she is and what she is meant to do. Every answer leads to another question that takes her closer to the truth behind her past and what darkness now awaits the future for her and everyone she loves.

Excited to have answers she has searched for her whole life; she soon questions if her life and everyone in it would have been safer if she had stayed home learning how to control her powers as her mother taught her all she would need to know to take over as the leader of the witches one day.

From discovering the truth about who her father is, finding love where she least expected it, and learning she is the key to giving the supernatural world the unity it needs, there is no shortage to the twists and turns.

Moonlight Changes (Book 2)

Amberly's life is anything but normal. Finding out the truth behind who she really was didn't even crack the surface of all the changes coming her way. Learning she is being hunted by someone hundreds of years old is the least of her problems. Dreamwalking into another shape-shifter mind that needs her help only adds to her troubled life. But when she starts having visions and seeing everyone, she loves dead at her feet she starts to scrabble against the clock. Wanting only to train, and become stronger, so that she can protect the ones she loves from their horrible fate. But can fate be stopped? However, the new shapeshifter isn't the only person she's dreamwalking with. She finds Vladimir's right hand, Aidan invading her mind more than once. Who is he? Why does he feel so familiar to her? While dealing with all the changes in her powers and turning eighteen, she's trying to find some stability in her life and her love life is anything but that. But catching Julian kissing the new girl is only the start of her world unraveling at the seams. How is she supposed to learn how to control her powers, learn to shift and defend herself when her heart is broken? Knowing Vladimir is coming for her and the ones she loves, she wipes away the tears and goes to work. She will do anything to make sure her vision doesn't come to pass.

Moonlight Legacy (Book 3)

Serenity:

It's all happening as I've seen in my dreams. Amberly learned who she was. Was united with those she should have known her entire life. Met her true mate. And then was torn from us all. But hope still springs, because in being lost, Amberly will find answers and learn the true strength of her heart. The last battle might have been lost, but the war has only just begun. And Amberly's choices from here on will send out ripples that will shape the future of our world. But can an eighteen-year-old choose the right path when darkness and grief obscures every way forward?

Enough is Enough

My name is Elena and I have put a plan in motion to escape my abuser and recurring nightmare. However, there is that old saying about the best-laid plans going awry... Escaping your abuser only to have new obstacles laid out in front of you. Now not only does my body need to heal but my mind as well. Beaten, torn down, and broken. I'm no longer the woman I once was and to find her again will be no easy task. Anxiety takes over my mind and body whenever any man gets too close. Even if it was someone I knew would never hurt me. Can I overcome this fear? Can I get close to a man again and live out the rest of my life in peace, or am I destined to be alone and afraid for the rest of my days? A story of a broken woman fighting to stabilize her life after ending her abuse. Can she silence the fears in her mind and allow herself a happy ending with her lifelong friend Jason, or will the anxiety and fear her husband beat into her win out? Jim has become Elena's living nightmare but today everything changes. Elena has put her plan in motion. A plan to take back both her life and happiness

Will's Awakening (Book 1 In the Dark Awakening Series)

Will Walker's life is about to change forever as destiny finds us all one way or another.

His life shattered to pieces the day his older brother West was murdered, and their father disappeared from his life overnight. His mother is the only person left in his life until his childhood best friends, Thea and Trey, fight to make amends.

Will is facing demons of his own that he fears he can't outrun and that may keep him from the normal life that he craves so badly.

He's being hunted in his dreams by the Company and their leader Morpheus and soon realizes that there was more to his brother's death than anyone knew, but Will holds a more profound secret.

Will soon discover he may be the only hope the world has against Morpheus. Will he be the world's savior or their doom?

www.ingramcontent.com/pod-product-compliance
Lightning Source LLC
Chambersburg PA
CBHW020339260626
47156CB00004B/1597